The audiobook for THE RIVER ROAD is now
available online where all major audiobooks are sold.

THE RIVER ROAD

Benjamin Boucvalt

Ghost Light Publishing

N E W   O R L E A N S

THE RIVER ROAD

Copyright © Benjamin Fulton Boucvalt, 2013
Published by Ghost Light Publishing

First edition: May, 2014
ISBN: 978-0-9903334-0-1

Front/spine cover illustrations by Andy Westhoff
westhoffenator.tumblr.com

Back cover illustration by Sophie Lucido Johnson
SophieLucidoJohnson.com

Design Consultant: Nick Tierce
NickTierce.com

Edited by Valerie Boucvalt
ValerieBoucvalt.com

For my wife,
who endured, who took a sledgehammer to the wall
fortifying my heart,
smashing it into oblivion, teaching me to fix the world
by fixing myself.

You are my heaven, and so be it, my hell.

With all my heart.

The River Road

TERRORS IN THE MOONLIGHT

The moon's solemn image painted on the black mirror of swamp water shattered as his body collapsed upon it. He rose, pushing himself through the knee high sludge until he fell again, frantically putting his back to the nearest tree, his heart beating to the bark. Looking back on the path he had come, there was no one. He saw a maze of cypress trees navigated only by a lingering white fog, a spirit whose translucent skin was pierced with the moonlight that had kept him alive this long. He sucked back air with each pounding pump of his heart. Eyes locked on his past. As the wind slithered through, it carried with it echoes of his plight, hissing a whispered scream in his ear, the hounds howling for his blood. His arms slowly rose from beside him dripping with the muck he had tried hard to fight.

A long strand of mud hung from his wrists, sliding back to the water, and as each clump fell it revealed the

1

chains that were shackled to his wrists. Broken. Free. His eyes moved to his hanging chains. A moment that seemed to silence the echoes was broken by a gust ripping through the ghostly fog at the cracking of a whip.

He was up once more, flying forth with what remained of his will, his arms shielding him from the tangles of the wood. As each foot plunged into the swamp there came a pull from its depths, swallowing his legs deeper and deeper, but he did not succumb. The swamp's yearning for his surrender was overcome and he rose out of the black, tearing through the night. The echoes on the wind began to fade as he slammed his foot onto solid ground. The silence twisted him around to look back. No one. Not even the looming fog. He spotted a pool of light cast out on the cold ground. He held his hand out to it, embracing the moon's light on his black skin, and then rose his other. Slowly he stepped inside the beams as he bathed his face in their caress. His eyes were closed while his mouth stretched wide revealing the white splendor of his smile. A slowed heartbeat inhaled the night sky. It gave him a warmth that was denied by the swamp moments ago. *Freedom,* he thought. His eyes opened to the broken chains before him. *Never again,* he thought. And as he stood in wonder, with this new life breathed into him from the heavens, a sharp crack rang out as a leather cord wrapped and constricted around his neck, yanking him from the moon's light back into the darkness, back to the ground of the swamp.

The whip went slack when his body slammed down. He choked and coughed and sucked for air. When it finally came, he saw before him a tall figure untouched by the light. The sharp black lines of his body were still like the cypress around him. He heard the figure's breath and saw it steam out of the shadows, thawing the night air. A dragon from his cave. It began to move and he shook, paralyzed by its presence. Merging into the moonlight rose a revolver aimed at the man's head.

His hands sprang to shield his face as he cried, "Please."

The light bounced off the long steel barrel back up to the face of the figure, revealing only a chin marred by a scar that rode along its stubbled jaw.

"Please."

He lowered his hands in hopes of receiving mercy. The gun slipped back into the shadows. He released the air held within him, looking to the figure that retreated. As he watched it move in the night, there, more silent than them all, a horse as black as the figure waited. A stoic servant of stone, whose eyelid blinked calmly over its glassy eye. The figure approached it pulling a rope from the saddle and walked back toward the man. It knelt down near him, tied the rope to the end of the whip that was still attached to his neck, stood and walked away.

"Sir?"

It threw the rope over a thick branch of a cypress, then back over to his horse, tying the other end to the saddle.

"Sir?!"

The figure signaled to his minion with a subtle click from his mouth, and the two moved away from him. Frantically he tried to unwrap the whip from his neck while the slack in the rope was disappearing. He tried to pull the beast back but it would not heed and the now tightened rope started to lift him off the ground.

The air that he fought so hard to hold onto had left him. His body hanged, gently swaying with the Spanish moss in the trees. The figure gazed. The dragon breathed while that haunted fog crept back in, consuming the body, accompanied by the echoes of his fears that hissed and wailed out in the forgotten places of this land.

WHAT MOST FORGET THE CURSED REMEMBER

The wagon squeaked as it bounced along the gravel road that followed the mangled bends of the river. He sat in the bed of the wagon leaning his back against a bail of hay, keeping the river behind him. A terrifying thing, that river is. A long arm struggling to find North. Her muddy water hiding what lies beneath. Her wide belly that tempts men to cross, waiting to pull those who can't endure below, swallowing them forever. He dared not look on her. She was always watching. Now, enough about his nightmares.

What he did look upon was a towering ocean of sugar cane. An ocean not because of its size, though it was quite immense, but because of the way the wind passed over its tops. They rippled and swayed as it blew through, resembling the ocean tide. Wave after wave the winds rolled. A mighty beautiful thing sugar cane is, its green and gold leaves bursting with life. Sweet, too. There's nothing quite like sitting under an oak sucking on a stalk of cane.

The wagon came to a halt. He looked around to see what it could have stopped for, but there was nothing in sight. Just the cane and the river. The driver turned from the front, chewing on a piece of cane, with its juice creeping down the side of his face. His beat and blistered hands pulled the cane from his mouth, "Just up the road, you can't miss it." The driver pointed down a white shell road.

"This way?" he asked, as he placed his cane on the ground and rolled gently off the back.

"That's it." Without hesitation, the driver hurried off, continuing on his way.

"Thank you, sir," he yelled back as the wagon vanished, leaving him in a cloud of dust. He doubted he was heard. The driver was an alright man, gave him a ride up there and all. Though the driver wouldn't let him sit up front on a cushioned bench, under a covering that shielded the blaze of the sun, it was more than he could say of most. They said times were changing. Hell, times are always changing. But for that time, the wagon bed would suit him just fine. The hot, splintered planks that had been baked in the afternoon sun were a much more comfortable place than to what he was accustomed.

The man stood at the mouth of the shell road and took his coat off, throwing it over his arm. His route would cut straight through the cane, enclosing him in ramparts of long stalks. It was the home of his birth. He never thought he'd find himself walking the River Road again, but you can only go so long without doing what you know is right. He started to walk the road listening to the cracking of the shells beneath his feet. He held his hand out to brush with his fingers the long green leaves of the cane, as if he was shaking the hand of someone he knew long ago. Holding a little longer than you normally would, staring into their eyes for just a moment more.

As the road came to a bend, he met a grey wood fence surrounding a cemetery. It was a fine square enclosure, not too big, as the area didn't have many people. The grander cemeteries were closer to town and were kept up a lot better. He walked through the gate of the fence and started to read the gravestones. He noticed that many of the men here had fought in the Civil War, back when he was much younger. He read *captain, lieutenant, private.* A lot of privates. In fact, most of the graves were for those of the rebellion, or their affiliates…save one. He spotted a wooden cross cast out from the others in the corner of the cemetery, buried in the shade of the trees. He still didn't know how he was able to go on without doing it, to have gone so long without saying goodbye.

He made his way toward the cross. Grass had grown wild around it, consuming the rotting wood that the earth continued to bury, making it one with itself again. The old man braced himself on his cane as he lowered himself to the ground. He ran his fingers along the name that time

7

had made barely visible. He kneeled above a man, one living in a world he didn't deserve, trapped and imprisoned. Like many others he'd known. Strangely, when he would stare into his reflection, burrowing into those dark eyes of his, they turned light. He saw the man below. He saw himself. What follows is the tale of the two of them. More like a myth, really. For that is the fate of a story born in the shadows, decayed by time.

THE PULL OF THE PAST

Snow, which wasn't strange for these parts in the spring, filled and rolled off the windowsill of the library. Inside the window were many opened and unopened books lain out on a table, taken from the hall of polished wooden shelves. He sat at the table among the books, buried in the back, almost hidden by the numerous rows of literature. Stillness was all around him as his green eyes gazed. Stoic and frozen. Fixed not on the books, but out the window, through the chilled glass that held back the biting air as he sat in the dark light of day. A young man stuck in a portrait of waiting. A man who would remain there still, even if the glass of the window exploded from the intense pressure of the cold. And as his skin covered with frost and the glass sliced his face, he would but blink.

A crescendo of clunks was heard in the place from approaching footsteps. Still he sat. Listening. As if he knew this oncoming thing would deliver him from this place that he had lingered for almost a decade. A place of paused progressions, of shallow studies, of faceless meetings frozen in time. A place that he'd be glad to stay. The footsteps finally stopped. He heard from behind him, "Ory." He turned to see a kind looking gentleman holding a letter by his side. "This came for you."

The gentleman extended the envelope to Ory, but he did not take it. Ory stared at its seal imprinted with *RR* in red wax. And the seal stared back at him. Amidst their stand off, the gentleman stood looking back and forth between the envelope and Ory. He broke it with, "Ahem."

Ory looked up to him, nodded, and took the letter. Breaking out of Ory's mouth, "Thank you."

It was the first time that Ory had spoken that day. The gentleman left as he turned back to his table, pushing the books aside, clearing his station, placing the letter out on the desk with the seal facing him. He didn't lock with it again, instead he avoided it. He pulled out a gold pocket watch and cradled it on the table. His thumb caressed its door. It circled and circled, polishing a shiny track around the rim of the gold, leaving the center dark. The watch clicked open. One side was its clock. Its hands didn't move. Stuck on no relevant time, just stopped. He had no memory of a time when it actually moved. The other side held the portrait of a woman. Ory looked upon it, but not as he did through the chilled glass or the rigid red wax. Her eyes bored into him, leaving him hollowed by the absence of hope, and his face yearned for a command or sign of what to do, but neither would come. And soon his eyes would drift from the portrait on to the red seal that continued its stare.

Ory reached out for the letter. He grabbed it. Held it. Felt it. He shook his head at it and with a deep breath broke the stare of the seal, pulled out the letter and read.

> *Before you toss this letter aside and send us back your prewritten response, know that I am not my father. He asked me to write in hopes that we might receive some new information about you and your wellbeing. I have seen your responses to my father's letters, or should I say response, as they are all the same. But it must be true then, that you are busy and the time isn't right, for you can't afford to write us anything new. Which I am sure is why I never received anything myself. Writing this makes me restless in these strange times. Yet, I find a sense of comfort in you, even after all these years. Do you still have hopes of our marriage? I am much different than you would remember. I have been educated like you and have grown a great deal. My father hopes that your answer is yes. He misses*

you and would be honored and privileged to see you again. I, too, hope, if it be your desire, that your answer is yes. Not for the plantation, or whatever rumors pass along the River Road, but for the love I bear you. Not because my father tells me I should, but because as I look back through my childhood eyes I see the light from the horizon burned in my memory with the image of an older boy before me. His smile as radiant as the sun. What was then a child's fantasy has grown into our destined reality. I told myself I would love that boy, and today, I am proud to say, I love that man. My father would hope that you'd reply with word of your homecoming. But the good that it would bring my father doesn't match the feeling it would bring me if just one word was changed in your identical letter and sent back, prolonging my most respectful wait.
Love, Bernice

Ory let the letter fall to the table as he sat back. His face was cold. He breathed. You could hear him. Breathing. He looked back to the portrait of the woman. Nothing. He turned back to the icy window and looked out to the dark sky, settling back in his portrait prison.

But before he entered again, the sun sliced through the clouds, its beams thawing the glass, shining on his face. His eyes would change, whether for good or bad could not be told, and while the light grew about him, the portrait of the woman began to grow brighter. Her face would soon burst into flames, but it was extinguished by the golden door as the watch clicked closed.

BARE KNUCKLES AND MOONSHINE

They were the Bertrans and this was their barn. Set alone just outside of town. From the outside it was quiet and peaceful, sitting in the night sky, but the cage that was this barn housed nothing of peace, nothing of quiet. Its walls held back most of the light burning from lanterns, allowing only some to seep through the wooden planks into the darkness. You could hear it, the closer you got, swelling inside its belly, muffled cheers and screams about to burst from its walls. Trapped inside was pleasure and pain.

Inside, at the edge of the barn's loft, the Bertrans sat. They were three brothers. The younger was Jacques, whose wide grin stretched across his weasel-like face, and Oak, whose nickname he got due to the fact that he was almost seven feet tall and his expression rarely changed, wide-eyed with an open mouth. Sitting between them was Jean Bertran, the eldest. Money clenched in his fist, biting his bottom lip, Jean loomed over the beauty that he saw below. A mob of drunk, greedy, and anxious white men crowded beneath them. Some stood shoulder to shoulder, some sat on bundles of hay, some climbed up to the loft where the brothers stayed. But most stood in the center, leaving an open circle, an empty space where their attention lay.

Inside this ring was a tall, thick, strong, black slave, kneeling on the ground with his shirt off. Sweat dripped from his body as his shoulders rose and fell with each deep breath he took. There was a slight shake about him. He turned and twitched at every sound and movement in the room, actions of prey cornered and toyed with. Across from him was another man, a slave in his similar state. Just as tall, but thinner. He was different, though. With him there was no shake. He knelt quiet and calm, breathing with indifference, a rise and fall of boredom and use. His name was Will. A man who seemed to accept, to have given in to his place, and he moved about disconnected from the world. But many would never know there was something that couldn't be seen, a faint roar deep within him.

Water was thrown on Will and the other slave as the crowd cheered. All around them, money and moonshine passed along down the river of hands circling them. Dollars were snatched and bottles were grabbed. A man yelled from up in the loft, "Come on, let's go."

Jean continued to look down with a calculating smile. The two men rose, and with them their bare knuckles. They began to close their distance. The one slave shuddered with each yell he heard around him, and the louder they got the bigger his shudders became, until he seemed to want to silence them all with his fist hurled at Will and a scream all his own.

Will evaded the assault with a duck under the swing, which only fueled the crowd's amusement. The waving of money and the urging from the crowd stole Will's focus. Another swing came flying at him but Will still managed to avoid it. The images began to flood Will's mind, the moonshine, the wide white man's mouth open in laughter. He heard, "Kill him!" Will squeezed his eyes and shook his head. Waving arms, dancing dollars, chains dangling from the barn walls.

Then all at once the images shattered when a bare fist slammed into Will's face sending him into the crowd. Jean stood up, with Jacques and Oak still by his side. "Yeah," he growled.

Will laid in the arms of his distractions, the flood of images fell away, save the one before him. A man waiting to strike him down again once he rose. As his vision sharpened and breath became deep, like the wild cat hidden in the tall grass approaching his prey, he exploded from the crowd and into the ring. Will swiftly moved under the swing of the man and buried one fist after another into his gut. The man cringed, dropping his

16

hands to hold the pain. Will took in his unprotected face and swung, a moonshine bottle dropped, he swung, blood on his bare knuckles, he swung, a man wailed, "No." Then he drew his fist back once more, and stopped. He looked upon the man's face now covered in red in hope that he might fall, but instead watched his arms slowly rise. Will's fist took speed again and the man collapsed to the ground.

Cries of acclaim and disappointment filled the barn. Jean remained standing in the loft. His smile had left him. Another man approached him and grabbed his money. The three brothers remained there hovering over the chaos. Jean looked at Will as the mob filled the circle engulfing the slaves below.

Will stood above the unconscious body, a juggernaut with fists of stone. He looked down on his victim as the shoulders of the men squeezed around them, over them. The fixated rage consuming Will faded, and that deep breath of a beast unmoved returned inside him. His eyes became soft and his fists loose hands. There was no sympathy, no regret. He remained as he was before. Detached. Wandering in what was to him a hollow shell of a man, a rotating cog of this machine moving neither forward nor backward, stuck between worlds, amidst the absence of time. Waiting.

RETURN OF THE SUN

The horse's hooves fell at the pace of a steady heartbeat as it stamped along the river with Ory mounted on its back, a pink sky above him, and as he rolled back his shoulders, lifting his head, he turned to catch the sun peek upon the horizon and there went dawn. He left the riverboat earlier that morning, one he had taken a far way's east and even further down to the South. Ory preferred his solitude in seeing this place again, a place most would have called home. Once that southbound river contorted toward the East, he knew he'd finish his journey by land. And so he did. Ahead of him he saw a black river turn brown and those all too familiar stalks of cane revealed under the morning light of the Southern sun.

He had been riding for hours, and with the coming of light, he watched the world wake. But on the River Road the first movements would not be the comforts of the privileged, but those of the machine. The churning of the slave. The edges of the sugar cane fields became lined and filled with black men and women. Cane knives crashing at the base of the stalks. The towers would fall, be hauled off and stacked in wagons.

A white man walked about them. Watching. Henri's yellow shirt, which used to be white, was gathering patches of sweat. It takes a certain man to sweat in a cool early morning sun while he watches other men work. He continued his watching, then noticed a slave sitting on the ground, cane knife beside him. Henri scratched the blonde stubble on his neck and approached the slave. Once he reached him, the shadow from Henri's head cast over the slave's face. The slave relaxed his squinting eyes, and just as he did so, Henri tilted his head, blasting the light back into the slave's face.

"Pick it up."

The slave stood and grabbed the cane knife.

"Give it to me."

He did. Henri stood for a moment, gripping the knife, staring at the slave, whose jaw hung in uncertainty. Then the knife shot up above Henri's head as if to come down on the slave. The slave crouched to protect himself, turning his face to the ground. After realizing he was still in one piece, the slave looked up to see Henri staring at him still, but no knife. It had been thrown off into the road.

"Pick it up."

The slave looked to the knife and ran for it, then ran back. Henri held his hand out for the knife. He took it from the slave again, cocked back, stared, then threw it again.

"Pick it up."

The slave looked at the knife, then Henri, then the knife.

"Pick...it...up."

In the road, right where the knife lay, Ory rode in and stopped over it. Henri and the slave looked at Ory. Ory noticed the knife below him. Henri turned from Ory back to the slave. Just as the slave's face turned back, Henri's hand slapped across it. Blood dripped from the slave's lip. As the slave approached Ory he took cautious steps. He bent down to retrieve the knife and when he turned, Ory noticed blood stains on the back of the slave's shirt. The slave tried to hand the knife back to Henri, but he nodded his head back toward the cane and the slave resumed his work. When Henri turned back to see Ory again, all he caught was his back slowly disappearing behind the cane. Henri wondered on that familiar face, and for some reason he knew, he would see the man again.

Ory continued along the road, thinking about what he saw without surprise. As he passed along, his attention pulled down to his hand that held the gold watch imprisoning the female portrait, and he admired its beauty. His gaze had a sense of comfort, then his eyes squinted, hit by an unseen blaze, and he turned his head from it, back to the road.

Still at a steady pace, Ory moved off the road, creeping away from the river. Small homes, each with its own little porch, appeared underneath the branches of enchanting oaks. Out in front of the homes, sitting on chairs and the steps of the porches, men and women relaxed and leisurely sat and waved as Ory passed by. A magical scene, where the tree's shadows seemed to cast a spell on the homes and the people that dwelled in them. Then he halted. The horse dug into the earth, shook his head, and neighed. Before him was a white wooden home, bigger than the others, with a porch that wrapped around half of the house, green shutters, and flowers planted at the bottom of the porch stairs. Ory looked on. A rocking chair swayed back and forth in the wind. Empty. He waited to watch it stop, but it didn't. It kept rocking with the breeze, or with the rhythm of a ghost sitting unseen, waiting for the return of a loved one who had lost their way home, putting the spirit to rest only when they found home again. The rocking continued, seeming to never end. Ory took in air, trying to find any reason to forget about what he saw, shook his head, rubbing his face with his hands. *It is just a chair in the wind*, he thought. Then yelling came from the side of the home, pulling Ory away from the ghostly rocker.

Ory approached the side and saw the Bertran boys, Jean, Jacques, and Oak, having a meeting where they were judge, jury, and executioner if need be, in what, in their minds, was a crime. The offender in this case was Will, who stood tall before them, as tall as one could stand in his circumstance. Oak towered next to him, as sort of a bailiff, with his hand around the back of Will's neck, as one would grab a misbehaving dog, his fingers almost reaching completely around. Jean questioned, "You know you broke his ribs?"

Will didn't respond. It was a good choice, most any answer to that question would appear to Jean as condescending.

"Where are the ribs, Jacques? About right here?"

Jean points to Will's ribs.

"Yeah. About there looks good."

Jacques laughed, which sparked laughter in Oak, as well, who resembled a hog desperate for air. Jean pulled back and punched Will in the ribs. Will breathed hard through the nose.

"Well, I was hoping that might make you cough up the money you cost me. Maybe it was his eye. You know what you did to his eye?" Jean punched Will in the face, then shook the sting out of his hand, "He can't see out of it presently."

Will's face rose with a cut under his eye. Jacques joined in, "Still not seeing that money, brother. Maybe we need to break his legs."

Jean turned to Jacques with disappointment in his eyes.

"He didn't break his legs."

"Well, does that matter?"

"Yes, it matters."

Will couldn't help but to release the slightest grin. As Jean turned back to Will, he caught the smirk just as it left Will's face. Jean moved right on top of him, ordering, "Oak." Oak's fingers began to squeeze down on Will's neck. Snapping his neck would seem as easy to Oak as cracking an egg. Jean observed his face, seeing if the smirk would return.

"I would have no problem seeing your eyes pop right out of your head. My guess is, though, you may be fighting again. When that happens, take the beating you deserve, or take it again from me."

Jean finished his sentence and Oak released Will from his clutch. Will stood unsure if he was to leave or stay, then Jean shooed him, "Go on. Get."

Ory, who had watched the whole case, dismounted his horse as Will approached. The crash of his spurs hitting the ground caught the attention of Will, and the Bertran boys, as well. Will stopped. The two looked at each other, and for the first time, they both appeared at ease, holding in this connection that time failed to destroy. And on a single shared breath, they moved closer, walking, almost mimicking the other, until they met, and stopped. Both searched for words, and they did for a while, until Will finally spoke.

"Did you get lost?"

"Lost?"

"It's been a long time."

"Yes," he smiled, "It's been a while."

They both shared in the smile and Ory raised his hand, with what Will thought to be a gesture to shake his hand, but it continued to rise and instead landed on Will's shoulder. Regardless, Will still found comfort in it.

"Good to see you, Will."

"You too, Master Ory."

Master Ory. Those words came out as naturally as any other he'd utter. They waded in this calm state a little more, then Ory noticed the blood trail of a single drop from Will's cut. It was so slow. He thought that its crawl would freeze, or judging by Will's current demeanor, Will could stop it and command it to be sucked back up into the wound.

"How's the eye?"

"I can still see."

Ory handed the reins to Will.

"Would you see this taken care of?"

"Yes, sir."

Ory walked toward the Bertrans who had remained there watching. During his approach he took his gloves off, rubbing the center of his hands. He never looked them in the eyes the entire walk. He just focused on his hands. Jean asked, "Can I help you?"

"Is this your property?"

"No."

Ory's eyes remained down. "Then why are you on it?"

Jean laughed, "I don't think I like your questions."

Ory slapped his face. Jean turned his red cheek back to Ory, now seeing those green eyes, marble stones on the verge of cracking. Ory repeated, "Then why are you on it?"

All three of the boys jolted back at the glare, not solely from the menace, but also from the familiarity.

Will, in the distance, still holding the horse, stalled his orders, enjoying the sight of this old memory sweep in. He watched on in subtle laughter.

"What did that nigger tell—" Another slap cut him off. Jean's head whipped to the side. He held his jaw and said slowly, "That boy cost me money."

"And you're costing me."

The confusion faded, the look of mystery was gone, venom returned to their eyes, and the boys realized who this was. Ory walked away. "Get off my land."

Jean yelled, "Ory?"

Turning back, "If I catch you around here again without legitimate cause or laying a hand on my property again…," Ory tilted his head down on them, "You understand me?"

"Yes."

"Yes, what?"

Biting his bottom lip, "Yes, sir."

As if to grant approval, Ory nodded, then walked toward the house.

Will, still standing with the horse, was no longer laughing. No longer amused. The feeling had been ripped from him. He took the horse by his side walking away and thought, *Property*.

Oak snarled above his brothers, waiting for the command to attack, but it was never given. Jean said, "Let's go." And they all slowly slipped away, stewing on this return.

With each step Ory took onto the porch came a gentle placement of his boot, and though the house stood strong, his climb was taken with the fragility owed to a structure that could crash down upon him. As he closed the distance, the door grew wider and he felt dizzy, swaying, careful not to fall into the wide door, a well that could swallow him. He stopped in front of it. Regained his control. Centering himself. *It's just a door*, he thought. Then he felt it. He didn't want to turn. He knew it was there. But a pull that couldn't be fought slowly rotated his head to the side and there it was, still swaying in the wind, rocking. That chair kept its steady rhythm. Its haunt. Ory turned away, caught his skipping breath, and embraced the well to escape the ghostly wind. Then he fell inside the home, and as he did so, that looming chair that refused to yield, became still. A sign that would only have taunted him, bringing vain relief, for it began to rock again.

EXACTLY AS EXPECTED

The wood floor creaked with each subtle shift of his weight. Standing in the front room, the closed door at his back, Ory took in the walls around him. He noticed the hat rack, the crack on the frame around the mirror, a smaller set of stairs than he remembered, and then finally landed on the hall right in front of him. Its narrow tunnel led to a door at the hall's end and Ory's eyes slowly drew to its knob. His breath began to chill. The worn brass knob appeared to turn, hypnotizing him. The walls around the hall became dark and the cold spread. He was unsure if he had been transported into a dream again, or if this time it was real. The air around him bit his face as light grew from under the door. Ory's eyes were growing wide until he was released from the hypnosis by voices coming from the kitchen. He looked to the base of the door again, and the light was gone.

Ory came to the entryway where he heard the voices, standing just outside it, slyly avoiding being seen. He watched a woman, with the help of her black slave, prepare a meal, and a young man about Ory's age standing aside talking with them, laughing. He knew them all. The woman was his Titaunt, his aunt. The slave was Millie, an older woman who had seen many days in that house. The younger gentleman was CJ, wearing a vest with a shiny badge pinned to it. The two women whirled around each other in a choreographed dance. Ory, slowly leaned in with a bittersweet smile, and brought them all to a freeze with, "Could I trouble any of you for a glass of water?"

When the ladies turned, his presence triggered two different physical reactions, but both came from the feeling of joy as Titaunt's smiling face turned to tears and Millie screamed, "You're here." Millie came to him, wrapped her arms around his neck, pulling him down to her level. "So good to have you home."

She grabbed Ory's arm and escorted him toward Titaunt, who stood still in the amazement of his arrival. As he got closer to her she held her arms out to him. "Come here, my baby." Titaunt did what she could to cradle this man twice her size. She pushed him back to lay her eyes on him. "Still so handsome." Laughing, "and you stink."

Ory nodded as the three of them laughed. CJ pulled Ory in for a hug. A tight squeeze as if to make up for the ones missed. CJ let him go, asking, "You're late. You know your party's tonight?"

Ory stepped back to catch up on each of their faces after that tornado of a hello. He looked to Millie.

"Millie. You haven't changed."

Millie smiled as Ory turned to Titaunt.

"Titaunt. You've changed."

CJ covered his face to hide his amusement, while Titaunt's jaw dropped as she slapped Ory's arm. Millie warned, "I'd be careful there, child. I don't care if you just got here."

Ory shook CJ's hand. "CJ."

"Excuse me." Pointing to his badge, "That's Deputy Clement."

"Of course."

"It was only a matter of time. It's in my blood."

Ory forced a smile at the world around him, one he could have predicted, outcomes and responsibilities handed out at birth. And these burdens and gifts that they inherit, Ory inherited as well, and though he fought against them, he still found himself bound by them. Some he could bless, some he could curse, and one just walked in the room.

All laughter and smiling ceased at the sound of chopped wood hitting the floor. Ory turned to see Will standing in the doorway holding a stack of wood, and next to him, a pile of wood at her feet, stood a young white girl. Sidonie. Hair back, standing as tall as Will's chest, a dirty face of a girl who greeted Ory with anything but the joy that he had been given thus far. She examined him, scanning him with disapproval. Ory walked closer to her and knelt.

"Hey, Sugar."

"Hey."

"You remember me, right?"

"I guess."

Ory looked around to see everyone lower their heads, finding it hard to look. Then in a burst, Sidonie was on top of Ory, tackling him to the floor. The silence broke at this sight, smiles returned to their faces, and the biggest one then lay on Sidonie.

"What took you so long?"

"My horse was too slow."

"Don't you lie to me. Will and I were just with that horse and he looked bored."

"Did he?"

"Don't move. I'll be right back." Sidonie darted off leaving them all behind.

Will placed the wood down. "The horse is up, sir."

"Thank you, Will."

Sidonie flew back in holding a small rifle. "Look what I got."

When Ory saw the rifle, it was as if another person entered the room.

"Titaunt tells me that it was yours. How about you show me how to shoot? People say they've never seen anyone better than you."

Titaunt, trying to pacify her excitement, "I'm sure Ory would like to eat first."

"Come on, Titaunt, please?"

Titaunt turned to Ory, searching for what to say. She found nothing. Ory appeased her, "Go to the back." Turning to Millie and Titaunt, "We won't be long."

Ory shook CJ's hand again. "I'll see you tonight, I'm sure."

CJ smiled, proud that his friend was back home, hoping to go back to the way things used to be. Sidonie vanished outside, and just before Ory could make it out, Titaunt grabbed his arm. Her face grew tired, she looked at him and said, "Be careful with her. She hasn't been feeling well lately." Searching, "She's been having these dreams."

Dreams. This did not come as a surprise to Ory. Sometimes Ory could find himself drifting from a dream into reality, and that may be one of the best ways to describe all the days he'd been gone.

"Don't worry. She'll be fine."

Insisting, "We just got to watch her, that's all. She's fragile. She was much younger than you when—"

"Dreams are just dreams, Titaunt. They'll go away."

Ory had known better, but he said it anyway, trying to bury her thought and put her at ease. He left her there,

Millie came to her side, and they went back to work in the kitchen.

Ory exited the back of the house, walking out to a border of woods and swamp, and Sidonie stood, rifle in hand, waiting with bottles already set up as targets in the distance. Ory stopped and admired her preparation. Sidonie blurted, "Did you see Bernice yet?"

Ory walked toward her. "I just got here, Sugar."

"Titaunt said your marriage was decided when you two were born."

"Something like that."

"You love her?"

Ory nodded to assure her.

"How did they know that when you were born?"

"They didn't."

"Then why make you get married?"

"Well, it was arranged for the sake of the River Road."

"So for the plantation? That seems dumb."

Ory was amused by her. They stood and thought about that a moment, then Sidonie looked out to the bottles and pulled up the rifle.

"If you marry her, are you going to leave me again?"

"No, Sugar."

"Good. Because I'll shoot you." Sidonie fired at the bottles, but none broke. "Man, I can't hit anything."

"Yeah," he said, teasing her.

Ory knelt down next to her. "Sugar, you can't hope you're going to hit it. Tell yourself now that you have no choice. The bottle is going to break."

Sidonie thought about that as Ory ordered, "Raise the gun."

Sidonie popped the rifle up as fast as she could.

"See your target."

She aimed.

Calming her, "Breathe in slowly."

She took a long breath.

"Now hold it in."

She did.

"Listen to me closely. Learn to find comfort in this difficult place. Pack it down deep. Make it still."

Her little, calm face turned red.

"Hold it in tight… Now squeeze."

A gunshot rang out, and the bottle in the distance exploded, as did the air from Sidonie.

"There you go."

Panting, "Told you I could hit it." Still trying to catch her breath, "That's hard, though, holding that in."

"You'll get used to it."

She tried to give the rifle to Ory. It hung out in front of him, a hand waiting for a shake.

"Let me see you do it."

"Not today."

Turning from Sidonie, Ory walked to the house, never turning back, vanishing inside. Sidonie stood, wondering about what she had said or did, but in her child mind, the matter left her, and she turned her attention back to one of the bottles in the distance, raising the gun to her shoulder.

Gathering focus, and on a slow inhale, she burrowed deep, and whatever it was she held inside, it got chewed up and spat out with her exhale, shattering the bottle.

BREAKING SPIRITS AND STAYING ALIVE

Will entered the stables set just behind Ory's home. He threw down a bail of hay on top of a nearby stack, and from above he could hear the smooth sound of a strumming guitar, accompanied by the harmonious hum of a friend and fellow slave. Sitting in the loft above him, Johnny hung his legs over the edge, guitar in his lap, playing away as Will went about his duties.

"You're going to lose that."

"No, I think they like hearing me play."

"When you're called to the house, maybe. Not out here."

Johnny didn't reply, he just kept humming and strumming, taking the gamble. Will grit his teeth and continued to stack. Johnny, still playing, "So, who's this Ory?"

"This is his house."

"Why haven't I ever seen him?"

"He left a while back."

"Well, I've been here a while."

Will stopped and stared at Johnny nonchalantly playing as they spoke. "It's been a long while."

Will was always keen to spot things that would cause trouble, but was even better at spotting stupidity.

"What's he like?"

"Do you mean, will he walk in here and break your neck by smashing that guitar on top of your head?" Johnny stopped playing, looking up to catch Will's hard warning as he finished. "No. I don't think he's like that." Continuing to stack, "But he still owns you."

Johnny took his guitar and hid it in the loft above, climbed down, and joined Will in the work with the hay. They settled in to a routine and Johnny started up again.

"You know, I often wonder if they could just take a moment to hear me play, I mean really listen, maybe they might just want me to play for them instead of working out here."

"That's a nice thought."

"Maybe this Ory fellow could pay me for it. Then I could buy my freedom."

"Talk like that Johnny, it'll get you in trouble."

Trying to inspire Will, "Yeah, but if they could just hear me—"

"It doesn't make much sense for them to pay a slave does it?"

Johnny's charged, upbeat energy dropped, giving in to what they both knew was true. Their lives had been decided for them. They would go about inside this world as they were, or perish outside of it. A thought familiar to many along the River Road. Johnny, turned to look outside the barn, he listened, and when he confirmed the only one near was Will, he moved in close to him and whispered,

"I think I found a way out of here."

Will stopped, intrigued by Johnny's new demeanor.

"The songs that I've been learning, there's more to them. They aren't just songs. They contain messages. These songs came from other slaves, and they heard from others, passed down who knows how many times, but by someone who wants us to find a way. The songs are maps. Routes to the North. To freedom."

Will turned from him, heading out of the stable, but Johnny was quick to grab him, holding him in. "That's not all. There's talk of safe houses. Places along the way where people are willing to help. They're called Conductors."

Will whipped around grabbing Johnny by the shirt, "Johnny, you're a nigger up there and you're a nigger down here, it's not going to make any difference." Will let him go and Johnny stood defeated, with all his sense of hope slowly slithering away. Will, standing in the pieces of a friend destroyed, "Just work, Johnny. Play the guitar when you can. And work."

And that's what he did. Johnny walked back over to the hay and started to stack, reinforcing the walls of his own prison as the thought of having a choice withered, accepting his world for what it was.

Will watched his friend broken by the truth, or the truth that Will had come to believe. And just as Ory could predict his life on the River Road, so could Will. They saw their entire lives before them, planned perfectly into the machine, born into a life they couldn't escape. And closing their eyes they could see the portrait of their lives painted over many years, shackled to their minds with chains. Chains destined to be broken.

PREPARING THE BEDTIME ANGELS

It all happened so fast. One might think Ory's arrival on this day was intentional, leaving no room for waiting at this home in anticipation, catapulted back into his obligations and promises that he had hidden from. There Ory stood, dutifully, with no time left, dressed up in clean clothing. A charcoal vest buttoned over a white shirt. Titaunt walked around him, making sure not to miss any slight imperfection. Just behind Ory was Will. He was cleaned up as well, wearing fine clothing that he kept moving around in, trying to find comfort.

"I think it might be better if you took someone else, Master Ory."

"It doesn't matter who I'm with, Will. Just as long as I'm seen with one of you."

Will, in contempt, nodded his head, and realized he was not going to be obliged. Titaunt took a few steps back, looked at him sharply one last time, and declared,

"There. Perfect." She pulled a red tie out from her waist pocket. "Just one more thing. Sidonie and I made this for you."

Titaunt tied it around Ory's neck. He noticed his initials, *O.L.F.*, stitched into the bottom of the tie. Proudly, Titaunt finished the knot, straightened it up, and tucked it inside his vest.

"Oh, it came out wonderful." Turning to Will, "We got you cleaned up nicely too, Will."

Still fidgeting, "Thank you, ma'am."

"The clothes feel nice?"

"Yes, ma'am."

"You sure?"

Assuring her, "Yes, ma'am."

Ory looked over to Will in his uncomfortable state. Then Ory coughed. He held his hand over his mouth and coughed harder. Titaunt leaned in, "Ory, are you alright?"

He coughed again, shook his head, coughed on a hum, then, like a spark into a flame, the cough gradually picked up frequency, and with each one came a louder hum, until the cough faded and the hum became a giggle, and the giggle erupted into laughter. Titaunt, seeing that he was okay, smiled and laughed as well. Ory looked to Will and the sight of him forced Ory into an uncontrollable spell. Will at first was not amused, but soon broke and gave in to the delightful contagion. Felicity passed between them in a circle of laughter that lasted a good, deserving, long while. It wouldn't be strange to think that that was the first time Ory had laughed in over a decade.

As Titaunt calmed down, "I wish your mother could see you now."

The laughter subsided. Ory coughed one last time, looked down to make sure he was still in order after the hysteria, raised his head and took a breath. "Me, too."

Ory kissed Titaunt on the cheek and entered a nearby room.

The sun had set, and in the room, Millie sat in candlelight next to Sidonie lying in a small bed. Millie was reading to Sidonie from the Bible, though it looked as though she had committed it to memory.

"For He will command His angels concerning you to guard you in all your ways. They will lift you up in their hands, so that you will not strike your foot against a stone…"

Millie turned to see Ory hovering over her at the door. She slowly closed the Bible, and before she walked out of the room, she caressed Sidonie's cheek. "Good night, child."

She passed Ory with a smile, graciously relinquishing the bedside to him. When she stepped outside of the room she saw Will standing at attention, waiting.

"You look nice."

"Thank you."

"Would you like me to read to you while you wait? I'm sure Titaunt won't mind."

"Sorry, but I don't think it's a good idea."

"And why not?"

Millie sat down in a chair not far from him in preparation to read, opening the Bible, searching for a passage.

"I'm supposed to wait, not listen to you read."

She looked up from the Bible.

"Is that so? That's what you're supposed to do? Wait?"

Millie waited for a response from Will, but didn't get one.

"Is that really why you don't want to hear it?"

"Millie, where did you get that book?"

"Well, it's Ory's family's—"

"And who taught you to read it?"

With pride, "Titaunt showed me, mostly. She wanted help with Sidonie."

"So, them."

She looked down to the Bible. "Yes."

"Then like I said, I'm supposed to wait."

Millie stood. "That's good. You wait. But know, every man has to find faith in something. If anything, in himself."

Millie retired, leaving Will still at attention, standing outside the door with his master inside. He watched her leave, and somewhere behind his dark eyes he wanted her to stay, but nothing of his outer being would have it.

On the other side of the door, Ory was now in the chair where Millie was before. Ory and Sidonie sat in quiet comfort enjoying each other's flame-flickered faces.

"Millie was telling me about the angels. Again." Ory smiled, pleasantly surprised by her charm. She continued, "I must have heard that one a hundred times."

She giggled for a moment, then they fell back into silence. She tried to remain calm and casual with what she said next. "You're the only one I can really remember. Titaunt thinks I remember everyone, but it's not true. I just don't want to worry her."

"That's nice of you."

"Still, the only memory I have of you, is a time when you were running with me. Holding me, the trees were flying by. You were playing with me, I guess. What did we used to do?"

"We played all the time, for certain." Thinking, "I would put you to bed."

"Like now?"

"Yes, I would lie with you until you fell asleep."

"Would you lie with me now?"

"You're a lot bigger than you were then."

"Please?"

Ory was hesitant, for the memories of her were few and fading. The years before he left all revolved around

44

his nightmares, which so happened to be the only years they were together as brother and sister. If the candle went out, he might have been able to put it off for another day, but it didn't, and he had to look upon her face. A face yearning for a memory. Ory got up and lay down beside her, fitting what he could of his tall body into a bed that she, too, was growing out of. Both on their backs, shoulder to shoulder, enjoying again the silent serenity.

"I had a dream about Ma," she said.

Ory stared at the ceiling ready to slip into a dream himself at the mention of their mother.

"It upsets me, because I know she's there, but I don't know what she looks like. Tell me about my mother."

Ory thought for a moment, hesitant to give her an image for fear of what it could become when she got older, what it would look like under the light of the truth. But she'd have to deal with that in time, regardless. He breathed deep, as they both gazed beyond the ceiling, through the roof, and into the night sky.

"She had long soft hair, a light brown. Eyes were green, sometimes blue, and they made you feel so safe. She was beautiful. She looked like you. And she loved you very much. There were times when you would cry and cry, and Ma would just rock you and say, 'It's going to be alright, Sugar. It'll be alright.' And then you'd stop. And she'd sing to you. She had such a pretty voice."

"What would she sing?"

Ory thought on this a moment. "I don't remember."

"Would you sing it to me now?"

"I am sorry. I can't."

Sidonie accepted this, happy with what he did remember. She turned over to her side and put her head on Ory's chest.

"Ory... Are you my angel?"

"Like one of Millie's angels?"

"I guess."

"I can be. If you want me to be."

"I'm worried, all the people I love, I feel it, are going to leave me."

Trying to comfort her, "I'm here now."

"And that scares me."

"It's going to be alright, Sugar."

Ory reached for her hand and held it. "It'll be alright."

He kissed the top of her head, still cradled by his chest, and it wouldn't be long until she slipped away into a deep sleep, feeling safe and protected in her brother's arms. Ory looked on, straight through to that night sky, and the place that he usually found himself in, that time-suspended, dream-like reality, was now a place growing dim as he was brightened by the old light of a role he had forgotten. Then a crack appeared in the black wall within him, a wall imprisoning the light. He whispered to himself, "I am a brother."

THE KISS OF THE COLD GROUND

The night was calm outside the home. A light fog floated just above the ground. The moon's glow lit the dirt road that passed just outside and into the darkness. As the front door flung open, Ory came out of it at a charged pace, Will following right behind him. Ory forged down the road, but Will was quick to catch up with him.

"Master Ory, I think we're heading the wrong way."

"Thank you, Will. But, no, we're not."

Will said no more and followed alongside him. He walked wondering where they could be going. This was not the way to the plantation, and they were headed away from the River Road. Regardless, they continued on at a brisk walk that Will thought could spring into a run at any moment. The trees blurred by and dissolved into the shadows. As more trees appeared around them, their branches shielded the moonlight from the road, until they

47

were walking blindly in the night. Will followed the best that he could, relying mostly on Ory's footsteps, but also on the occasional glimpse of his white sleeve passing in and out of the darkness, like the coming and going of a light from the coast, guiding travelers.

Soon Will could see moonlight ahead of him. The trees scattered, and shortly after opened into a clearing bathed in a pale gloom. Will saw what they were coming to, and he knew well why they were there. It was a graveyard. They entered it at that same thunderous pace they had kept all the way there. Passing tombstones as fast as they did the trees, not looking at any of them. Will got the feeling they were close, he slowed his pace, distance grew between Ory and him, and a few more thunderous strides later, Ory came to a halt. At his feet was a tombstone, and chiseled into the cold stone was, *To our beloved mother, wait for us in heaven.* Ory pulled out his watch, clicked it open, and looked upon the lady in the portrait. As the clock remained in its dead, motionless state, the image of the woman seemed to turn, filling Ory's eyes with a cloudy haze.

Then, as he did back in his time up North, he became locked in a frozen prison, then came the blaze and all he could see went white and blew out. As sight came back to him, he saw himself much younger, standing at the end of a long tunnel, and on the other side, at the tunnel's end, a door. Ory felt a pull, one he stopped fighting long ago, that raised his arm and guided him toward the brass knob. In the light from under the door a shadow moved. He slowly glided toward this portal that muffled faint screams. They were the terrors of a woman and the tears of a child. Ory's hand reached out for the knob, gripped it, and turned, and when he did, that same blaze that delivered him from reality, yanked him right out of this twilight as he felt a hand on his shoulder and heard, "Master Ory?"

Ory turned to see Will behind him, who was concerned by the sight of his frozen appearance. Ory looked back to the grave, knelt down in front of it, kissed his palm, and placed it on the cold ground, holding the hand of the earth. He stood, closed the watch, and put it in his pocket. As Ory was preparing himself to leave, Will suggested, "We still have time, Master Ory, if you want to say a prayer or something."

Without hesitation, Ory turned and walked away. "No time for nonsense, Will."

Will wasn't fond of prayer, but he thought it to be their custom. Maybe it was a part of Millie that lingered in him from earlier that night. But in that moment, when Will stood and looked upon Ory's static state, he understood him. Will didn't know what he thought on. He didn't have to. All he knew was that he'd seen himself like that before, and was surprised by the subtle compassion that he felt for him.

And just like that they were off again, back toward the River Road. Once they found it, it would guide them to their destination, to an overwhelming force that lived upon it. The place where all the letters were written and sent up the river to find him, urging him and finally reaching with its long arm pulling him back down to its mouth. And for Ory, once he got there, it would try to swallow him, saying, *Welcome home.*

THE GIRL HE REMEMBERED

Ory and Will had been walking for a while now. Will noticed that the two of them were walking side by side. He didn't think too much on it, but he was used to always walking behind everyone, which is how they started out, but slowly their different rhythms merged, and they were moving steadily together along the River Road.

They heard it before they could see it. The bends in the river and its levee alongside it made it so that you couldn't see anything down the road until you turned. They followed the water and would be right on top of the plantation before they even knew they were there. Echoes of laughter and music slowly reached them as they passed along, growing louder until they made their final turn. Then, as if the levee and trees were stepping aside to unveil their destination, Ory and Will stopped in the middle of the road, and before them was the River Road Plantation. It had enormous white columns with a double

51

staircase coming down the middle, a porch that covered all sides, and on the porch were guests clad in the finest of clothes, lit by the golden light that poured from the windows of the plantation. Ory and Will walked until they reached the bottom of one of the staircases. Ory put his hand on the railing and stopped again. He looked down and saw that he already had one foot on the stairs. Will, still right beside him said, "I don't suppose we can turn back, Master Ory."

Ory shook his head no, and they went up the stairs, climbing to their destination.

When they reached the top, they approached two monolithic doors that were slowly opening, as if they had been waiting for them, and they walked inside.

The plantation was warm and pleasant. Guests filled the area, rubbing sleeves together as they all squeezed by each other maneuvering around the place. A band, all dressed in black, grouped in a corner with their stringed instruments, played as the guests continued their dance of mingling.

When Ory and Will entered, contagious looks and whispers bounced from face to face of each of the guests. Will, at this point, didn't mind falling behind. Ory stood tall as he was gawked at. From behind him Ory heard, "Took you long enough."

It was Titaunt, dressed far more elegantly than she was earlier that day, one made for this world under the glitter and glamour of the plantation. Her dress fanned out wide and her hair was done up. Around her bare neck hung a silver magnolia with small chips of diamonds in the center. It was around Titaunt's neck earlier, but Ory didn't notice it. Until that moment.

"We wanted to take our time."

Titaunt was proud to be at Ory's side, and as she smiled at those who took notice of her, she didn't catch Ory's prolonged stare at the jewel around her neck.

They walked through the crowd as a woman headed toward them, pushing people aside.

"Excuse me, excuse me."

Mrs. Lasseigne sprung out in front of them, coming to a halt with a slight shake about her, as if she could scream at any moment.

"I can't believe you're finally here." Looking for the words, "We're all very excited."

Ory graciously smiled and said, "You and your husband can really put on a party. You've done too much."

"No, nothing is too much for you. This is the homecoming of our future son."

Titaunt quickly corrected her, "My son."

"Yes, Titaunt. Figuratively, of course."

The second Mrs. Lasseigne said it, she knew she'd hear something from Titaunt, possibly even knowing the very response she'd give. Titaunt had become protective of Ory and Sidonie ever since she was charged with looking after them. What was first an obligation, turned into a burden, then into a badge she wore, explaining to the world why she didn't have a family of her own. It was the virtuous life that she settled for living.

Ory's gratitude could be seen in his expression, though his smile seemed to weaken, which wouldn't matter much as it completely deteriorated upon hearing the sound of a voice not far. A voice that drowned out all others as its singing grew louder. Mrs. Lasseigne watched Ory as he searched for the sound of the siren, and she picked up the smile that he had lost. Titaunt was apprehensive about him leaving her side, but she didn't stop him. Ory weaved through the crowd catching glimpses of a lady in the distance. Two hands in white gloves held together at her waist, he got closer, long brown hair pinned up exposing the back of her neck, he pushed a gentlemen aside, a long white dress, then Ory reached the edge of the crowd just as she turned, seeing her face, her eyes were that of a storm that refused to rage. It was Bernice, the girl from the letter that pulled him back. Ory didn't move anymore, managing to go unnoticed as she finished her song.

The silent crowd erupted in applause. Bernice, a little rosy, bowed her head gently, but when she lifted it, she caught Ory's eyes as he stood in the crowd. After a moment's daze, with a slight shake, she stood taller than before, chin a little higher. Ory walked to her with small, careful steps, and after a few, Bernice did the same. As this happened, the crowd around them slowly pushed away with each step the two got closer, until they met. They were alone in the middle of the floor. It was a time that was usually filled with cordial greetings, kissing hands, and with bows and curtsies, but they did none of these. For them, the guests who looked upon them faded away. While Ory looked he saw the start of a future with a girl from long ago, a friend turned into a beautiful woman, and inside the confines of her eyes he saw a glimmer of just the two of them somewhere outside this columned cage, a flash of happiness. And when Bernice looked back at him she saw her dream walk into her life, the boy she knew long ago having come back to her a man. She had been waiting and preparing in fear for this moment, one that filled her with an excitement that swiftly turned to terror.

The crowd wondered if the two were going to do anything, or say anything. Ory and Bernice continued in their childlike gaze, when from the balcony above, Cogan appeared, looking down upon them. The balding gentleman was Bernice's father, the one who had written Ory for many years. He walked to the railing and commanded the room, "Excuse me, everyone. I think it is time our couple shared a dance."

This broke the two from their trance, and both of them appreciated it, as they could have been stuck there for a while. The strings started to play, Ory held his hand out for Bernice's, and as that white glove slid into his hand, he guided her to the center of the room, where they moved with the music at an easeful pace. The crowd went back to their business, talking amongst themselves. Bernice, engaged in this dance, released from the hold Ory had on her, found it hard to look at him, keeping her eyes toward the floor.

"I got your letter."

Now looking up to Ory, "Oh?"

Ory thought that this might spark conversation, but was now at a loss for words.

"Was it different up North?"

"It was cold."

"Cold?"

"Yeah."

"That's all?"

"It was really cold."

Smiling, "And the ladies there, how were they?"

Ory thought for a moment. "Cold."

Bernice giggled and all her courteous actions were becoming genuine.

All the slaves that were working the party or had accompanied their masters stood lining the walls around the room. Will watched Ory dance while he stood at attention in this arbitrary formation. One of the guests, holding what was obviously not his first glass of wine, approached Will.

"You look familiar, boy. Where have I seen you?"

Keeping his eyes forward, "I don't know, sir."

"Yeah, I knew it." After another sip, "I saw you the other night." The guest looked around to see if anyone was watching and moved in closer to Will. "You did good, too." Patting him on the shoulder, "But just be glad you weren't fighting a white man, right?"

"Yes, sir, you're right."

The guest patted him one last hard time on the back and walked off laughing. Will stood still in his position, as he was before, back to watching Ory.

Ory continued to dance with Bernice, never noticing Will's conversation with the guest. He did, however, notice someone he'd just seen earlier that day from the cane fields. Henri, who was standing near Cogan. Up on the balcony, Henri and a group of other men were escorting a gentleman down the stairs. His name was Harvey, and as the men pushed him along, forcing him down, he yelled, "Get your hands off me." Looking back up to Cogan, "Fine hospitality."

Ory watched CJ rush to the bottom of the stairs to help the men push Harvey out of the plantation. Henri went back to Cogan, who shook his hand and slapped him on the shoulder, like Cogan would congratulate a child for a job well done. Ory stopped looking at them and asked Bernice, "Is that Henri Bertran?"

"Yes."

"Who was that man?"

"Harvey Sherman. He lives in the city. He was here to talk to my father about some political things."

"Political things?"

"That's what they tell me. What I've heard elsewhere, people think he's one of those abolitionists."

Ory got lost in thought as he looked on Cogan and Henri, but Bernice snapped him out of it with, "I heard you saw Jean this morning."

Finding no way around it, "Yes, I did."

"Did it feel good?"

"What do you mean?"

"Man, I bet it felt good. What I wouldn't give…"

As Bernice wondered, Ory was taken aback as she vicariously lived that moment behind her eyes, and he found comfort in the fact that the girl from many years ago was cloaked inside the woman before him, hidden behind the songs and white gloves of tradition and obligation. Her eyes drifted back to find Ory's, they picked up their tempo, and finished out their song in laughter.

The dance came to an end and the couple bowed to each other. Right on cue, Cogan announced from above, "Ladies and gentlemen…the future Mr. and Mrs. Ory Fortune."

The crowd roared and the place rumbled as the long expected marriage was finally getting under way. Cogan waved Ory up to the top of the balcony. Amidst the cheers and clapping, Ory looked again to Bernice who was smiling. She was settling in to the idea that maybe it could happen, her dreams could be reality, and as Ory walked up the stairs to meet her father, bombarded with pats and handshakes, she watched him as that terrifying sense left her with each step he took.

Ory had reached Cogan at the top of the stairs and was pulled in for a hug that sent the crowd again into a cheer. Cogan, put his hand to the side of Ory's neck, pulled their foreheads together, then kissed him upon it. Ory stood back, as if bursting from water, coming up for air. Cogan held his hands up trying to calm the crowd.

"The Best Man has requested that I give a toast on his behalf. As if I wasn't going to give one anyway."

Ory looked down to the bottom of the stairs and saw CJ, who held up a glass to him, as they exchanged a nod. Ory thought, *I guess I would have chosen him for my Best Man*. Cogan put his arm around Ory pushing him close to the railing, placing him on display.

"Soon I will be giving my only daughter away to a man I promised her to on the day he was born, years before my daughter was even born. Which is not easy for a father to do. But his mother and I decided it was for the best. Like a son, I saw him grow, and though he has been away from us for far too long, I have never doubted the man that he would turn into today. His mother raised a fine boy. And after many, many years of studying," chuckles came from the crowd, "he has returned to us a man. To fulfill the long awaited union of this land."

Turning to Ory, making an oath, "Ory, my daughter loves you, my wife loves you, I love you, and your mother loved you. I want you to know, in front of everyone here today...this is the best decision of my life." Cogan let that sit with Ory and the guests for a moment, then said, "So let's raise our glasses to a marriage that will make this place one, and to Ory."

The guests exploded in the biggest applause of the night. Cogan grabbed Ory's hand and raised it, like a fighter in a ring, and though it seemed impossible, the cheers became even louder. As the ovation continued, Cogan pulled Ory in again. Ory felt Cogan's embrace to be a little tighter this time, and as the seconds went by, Cogan's arms seemed to constrict. Soon the noise became unbearable and he could no longer tell if there were cheers or screams around him. All they had become was a vibration rolling around in his head looking for balance. And that high pitched buzz was the perfect accompaniment for Cogan's low smooth voice, when he lifted his mouth to Ory's ear and whispered, "Welcome home."

Cogan squeezed him one last time and they both turned out to the crowd that was finally settling. Ory took a breath and forced his usual smile. Cogan finished his final wave and stood in pride of a job well done.

The party continued, guests came up to the two of them, congratulating Ory and praising Cogan's speech, which, surprisingly, Cogan slowly walked away from.

Cogan's attention was caught by the only dark corner in the plantation, inside a small parlor in the distance. He peered into it, searching for those inside. The black silhouettes hardly moved. And as he looked closer, he saw a spark light up into a flame and vanish, then slowly floating out of the dark parlor came smoke from a breathing ember. Near the darkness was a room, and Cogan watched its door open and the figures slowly enter it. There were three of them. Two men and a shadow.

CLOAKED BY A SHADOW

Cogan walked in and two men were sitting in the chairs in front of his desk. Their clothes were weathered, small tears on their sleeves, and their boots had flakes of mud cracking off. Cogan made his way around them and sat at his desk. In his chair he faced the two men, and behind them, the open door to the party. Cogan looked on the verge of saying something when the door began to close, pushed from behind by a man in clothes of ash. Keeping his head low, shielding his face with the black brim of his hat, he turned his back to Cogan as he closed the door to a crack, and looked through it, watching the guests. Cogan looked back to the men in the chairs, waited for them to speak, then, "Did you get him?"

In a slow nod, "Yeah, we got him. He ran far. Furthest one has ever gotten."

"Good. We'll need to make an example of him in front of the others."

The two men looked at each other, trying to decide who would speak, until the other finally continued, "Well, sir, we got him but…"

"But what?"

"We found him in the swamp. Drowned, most likely."

"Drowned?"

Cogan looked back and forth between the two. Neither of them said more. He glanced to the man at the door who still had his back to them, as he peered through the crack. The man's eyes were caught by a woman who kindled his memory. The woman wearing a magnolia jewel around her neck. The man was staring at Titaunt, breathing in through his nose as if he could smell her in the distance. Cogan yelled from his desk, "Lezin, what happened?"

Lezin continued to gaze through the crack in the door without turning to Cogan, "You know how they are, Mr. Lasseigne. He turned violent. Tried to kill us. Had to be put down."

"Suppose I do."

Cogan bounced his head in thought. He looked back to the two men, "You can leave."

The men slowly put their hats on, stood and walked out the door. Lezin opened and closed it for them without taking his eyes off the party, and settled back into his former position looking through the crack again. As he peered through, his eyes that sat deep in his skull, looked at Ory. He watched how the different men and women approached him with smiles, and each smile that was given to him brought Lezin's eyes deeper into the caves of his sockets, growing darker.

"Lezin. Sit for a moment."

Lezin didn't move. He was fixed on Ory until Cogan raised his voice.

"Lezin."

With a quick whip of his head, like a serpent cocked back to strike, Lezin turned to face Cogan, but not in anger, or frustration, or annoyance. That's how he moved. Now lit by the light of Cogan's office was his stubbled face, and where hair no longer grew, that scar that traveled down the side of his chin. Cogan insisted, "Sit."

Lezin closed the door fully and sat down in one of the chairs in front of Cogan, sinking comfortably into the leather seat, pondering as he leaned back and crossed his legs.

"Harvey Sherman," Cogan stated. "He left earlier. Pleasant man. I'm going to need you to confirm his intentions for me. Then make sure he finds new ones."

Lezin didn't say anything or move at all.

Cogan, seeming satisfied, "Good." And on that, Cogan got up and went to a small bar underneath a book shelf on the side wall. He poured two glasses of a fine bourbon, and scooped out small, melting pieces of precious, rare ice from a small container built into the bar, then dumped them into the glasses. He brought one to

Lezin, then walked over to the door, cracked it open, and looked out to the party. To Ory.

"He's back. Things can finally get underway."

Breaking his silence, "It's not what she would have wanted."

"Of course it is."

"No it's not. Not like this."

Cogan left the cracked door, but didn't return to his desk, instead he sat in the chair next to Lezin, falling back, reclining.

"Everything's still the same. Ory inherited this land, and the plantation needs that land, and once he marries Bernice, it will be my land. The River Road needs room to spread and grow. She may no longer be with us, but this is what she wanted."

"She wouldn't want him to have it."

Brushing off what he said, "Lezin, I don't think you —"

"Don't tell me what I know."

Cogan stopped smiling and calculated what he said next.

"I just think it's best that you don't make this personal, that's all."

Silence fell on them. Not hearing anything else from Lezin, Cogan went back to enjoying the comfort of his chair, thinking the conversation was over, until Lezin, just above a whisper, said, "He looks just like his father."

Cogan didn't look to Lezin when he heard that. In fact, he avoided him, and just continued to empty his glass. But he could feel a chill coming from the man next to him. Lezin sat with his glass held out on his knee, as his expensive ice melted in a fine bourbon unsipped.

Ory, holding himself up from falling in social exhaustion, continued thanks and smiles, and smiles and thanks. He looked upon forgotten faces that were pulled out from the lost parts of his memory and right into the flesh in front of him. Babies had become children, children parents, parents grand-parents, and old names mentioned of those dead and gone. Eventually he made his way through the crowd, finally reaching the door to Cogan's office. He stopped, fixed his clothes, then reached for the knob. Just before he grabbed it, an arm flew between him and the door, blocking his entrance. It was Henri, who, at this point, smelled of moonshine, which wasn't served at the plantation, and judging by the used bottle in his hand, probably was made in his own home, explaining the awful stench.

"I knew you looked familiar. Sorry I didn't say anything out in the fields. Busy, you know?"

"Of course. It's fine."

"So where are you coming from again?"

"North."

"How about them niggers up there?"

Henri's face came in close to Ory, and he turned away just in time to save himself from being hit by Henri's breath.

"The same."

"Ha. Knew it. You can dress them different, but they're still niggers. Not one different from another."

"Excuse me."

Ory moved to enter the office but Henri put his body in front of Ory while feeding himself from his bottle. Henri wiped his face with his sleeve.

"You have a problem with my boys, Ory?"

"No, sir."

"You know, there's nothing wrong with reminding them who's boss."

"Absolutely. When it's your property. Not mine."

Henri smiled, tilted his head, and dug his eyes into Ory. "That's fine. As long as you don't have plans to be changing things. Guys like that pass through all the time and they always end up on the oak."

"Not looking to change anything."

Henri dropped his arm, moved out of Ory's way, and sank back into the sea of people. Ory stood and watched him as he disappeared into the deep. Ory thought that he was maybe too harsh with Jean upon his arrival. Maybe what he wanted Jean to know could have been said with words, and not the back of his hand. He tried to think what set him off. It was his property, yes, but something else rolled around inside him, building pressure, looking for a way out, and maybe that was just a moment where it tried to break free. It just so happened to be on Jean's face. What scared him the most was that, if that was just a flash of what was inside himself, what would happen when it all broke lose.

The thought had left him and he was back standing in front of Cogan's office trying to remember why he was about to enter it. To say thank you, mostly. It'd be the cordial thing to do. It'd be what was expected. And just before his mind found reason not to, he pushed himself through. When the door opened, Lezin and Cogan were still sitting quietly. Only Cogan turned to see Ory. Lezin kept sitting as the water from the side of his formerly chilled glass dripped down his leg. He knew it was Ory.

Cogan got up, "Ory."

"I'm sorry. I should have knocked. Feeling a little flustered at the moment."

Cogan came over to Ory, quickly moving him away from Lezin.

"Enjoying yourself?"

"Yes, sir. I wanted to thank you. This is more than one could ask."

Ory noticed Lezin still sitting in the chair, unmoved.

"If you are busy, sir, I'm sure I'll see you later."

Cogan grabbed Ory's arm, moving him toward the door, and whispered, "You know, that might be—"

Lezin stood. They stopped. Lezin turned around and walked toward Ory, but kept his head down. Ory couldn't see his face, and as he got closer, he first became worried, feeling in danger, but then felt at ease, then completely uncertain right as Lezin stopped in front of him. He tilted his shielded face up and Ory beheld Lezin's eyes sitting in the shadow of his face. They were locked in a stare that sent Ory into a state similar to that of his dreams, drifting from reality. Cogan, standing outside their world, tried to break them loose.

"Not sure if you remember Lezin."

Ory's eyes shook free, then he tried to register what he said as Cogan continued, "He was a friend of your mother's."

"No, I don't."

Ory held his hand out, but Lezin didn't take it. All he did was look down at it, then back up to Ory.

"Well, I'm sure you'll find time to get to know each other."

Before Ory withdrew his hand, Lezin placed the warm, watered down glass of bourbon into it and said, "It's just right."

The glass almost slipped out of Ory's hand from the condensation, but he was able to quickly grasp it. They looked at each other for another moment. This time, Ory didn't feel trapped. Something else caught him. Something behind Lezin's dark eyes began to pull another memory from Ory's mind, but just before it appeared, Lezin had made his way to the door and out of the office. He never said another word and the memory slowly slipped back into the mystery of his mind.

Trying to extinguish the awkwardness, "Don't mind him. He's seen tough times."

"He looks familiar. How do I know him again?"

Cogan had already moved from his side, not wanting to stand anymore where that strange encounter took place.

"Come see. I want to show you something." He went to his desk, searching underneath it. Ory looked at the letters stacked on it. Next to it were bars of red wax and a seal stamp for pressing the letters *RR* into their red melted form. Ory had broken many of those seals. Cogan pulled out a wrapped box from underneath the desk and smiled. He looked at Ory with anticipation. "I know I should wait to give this to you at the wedding, but I can't."

Ory watched as Cogan placed the box on the desk and pushed it toward him. As it got closer to him, he felt dizzy, as he seemed to do with many encounters on the plantation.

"Go ahead, open it."

Ory hesitated for a moment, looked up to Cogan who gestured for him to proceed, then pulled the box closer and opened the lid. He reached inside and pulled out two Colt revolvers. They sparkled in the light reflecting every candle in the room along their polished steel barrels.

Golden etchings ran around the handle, around the trigger, and down the barrel.

"Those are something, aren't they? One of a kind. Made specially for you."

Cogan couldn't have said anything more perfect or more in sync. Ory's entire life had been specially made for him. And that thought would pass over Ory as he cradled the revolvers in his hands. They felt comfortable and light in their making, smooth to the touch, but in his hands they grew heavy and coarse, weakening him by their weight. He placed them back in the box.

"Sir…"

Ory stalled in his thought as Cogan moved around his desk and came to meet him. He pulled out from the box a harness for the weapons. He held it out like a shirt and dressed Ory in it, having him put his arms through the straps, then worked on him as a tailor would a suit.

"You know, Ory. I want you to know, I'm not going anywhere. You take your time in this transition."

"Thank you, sir."

"Great things are waiting for you, whenever you're ready to take them."

Cogan tightened the straps and made sure they were secure. The next thing he would say he would take extreme caution with.

"I remember how you and your father would shoot all the time. What a great shot you were."

One would think that Ory would have done something here, but he did nothing. He didn't shake, get dizzy, or fall into any dreamlike state.

"You were the happiest I'd ever seen. That's how I knew these would be perfect."

Still nothing. Ory remained as if Cogan had said something with no meaning, in a language that Ory did not understand. The mention of his father bounced off him like a bullet would steel. If it did anything, it would fill the cracks in the black wall around his soul, sealing any leaks of light. Cogan took the revolvers and placed them in the holsters, which hung just under Ory's arms and against his ribs. After a few final adjustments, Cogan stepped back and looked at how well he dressed Ory in his gift. "Magnificent."

"They're beautiful, sir."

Cogan put his hands to Ory's cheeks, "Great things, my boy. Great things."

Ory could see the pride in his eyes. Maybe a sinful pride, but pride none the less. Ory saw what he was trying to do, but there was no place reserved for a father in his life. And as each moment passed in the plantation, Ory knew he was getting deeper. With each gift, with each speech, even Cogan's daughter, he was embracing this world, and with them would be forced to embrace all the things that came with it. Including his past. And that very well could have been the quest he was on. Perhaps a quest for self-destruction. As different elements came back into his life, so would come things he never knew, things that were always there, disguised in his mind. He'd be forced to face all those demons he hid from, and the ones hiding from him in the shadows of his past, ones that did not rejoice in his return.

THOSE WHO WAIT

From outside the plantation the music softened and the guests sporadically left. Ory escorted Bernice through the front doors and onto the porch. Will followed right behind them. From the porch they were high enough to see the river. Bernice held on to Ory's arm as they watched the moon's image dissolve and reappear in the water as each breeze passed along its surface. Ory thought about his journey up and down that river, and now with Bernice on his arm, he wondered if he'd ever leave again. He looked for a reason to think maybe this would be okay, that he could be happy.

Bernice turned from the river and let go of his arm. They smiled and knew it was time to say goodbye. She asked, "So, I'll see you tomorrow?"

"I'm sure."

Will watched as the two stood, each waiting for the other to make a move, but unsure of what the other expected. Ory had only been back a day and the wedding was already underway. Surely it would be acceptable. Bernice looked at him with all her might, saying everything she could without saying it, *Kiss me.* Ory leaned in. *It's happening,* she thought, *Just as I saw it.* Then Ory grabbed her hand and raised it to his lips and kissed it. Bernice, unsatisfied, wanted so much to break cordial code and grab him and do it herself. Instead she smiled, and in her elegance, swayed back into the plantation.

Ory and Will walked down the stairs of the of porch, Ory thinking that maybe he made a mistake, and Will said, "Pardon me for saying, Master Ory. But I think you made a mistake."

"I think you may be right about that."

They shared a laugh, enjoying the comfort of each other's presence. Ory looked out to the fogless night air, thinking of Bernice and her charm.

"You go on ahead, Will. I'm going to walk home alone."

"Yes, sir."

Will walked off ahead of him, fading into the darkness of the road. Ory waited there for a while. Guests still appeared here and there, many wives holding their drunk husbands up as the husbands attempted to escort them. They all looked as if they had the best of times. When they were all gone, Ory began to leave the plantation, he made but two steps and heard someone behind him.

"It's exhausting trying to look so happy."

Ory turned and saw Millie sitting on the porch. "Millie. Why are you here?"

"I'm always here."

It was an ignorant question. Ignorant because he was genuinely asking her about her choice to do something. The answer would always be the reason of someone else. Ory didn't remember Millie so much as a slave, but as someone who cared for him during his younger years.

"I was sent to help clean up after the party."

Ory, trying to make himself leave, intended to continue down the stairs, but he decided to stay with Millie to enjoy the night a little more. The two looked at the river as a few dark clouds blocked the moon's light. Millie said, "She's changed."

"She has. I only remember a little."

"Like what?"

"Just… She was much younger. Dirtier I guess."

Millie laughed. Ory tried to think back on her and all he could recall were the times a younger girl would chase after him and his friends in their teenage years, trying to keep up. Dirty face. Hair in the wind.

"She's still in there."

"I just want this to be what she wants."

Ory knew, that just as he had no decision, neither did she, and it would only be luck if they ended up loving one another. And maybe Ory would be lucky enough. But it was not satisfying when Millie declared, "Don't worry, It's all a part of the plan."

Ory stopped smiling. Even Millie, a slave, saw the design, reminding him of how this whole engagement was hollow. But Ory humored her.

"What plan?"

"Why God's, of course."

Sighing and under his breath, "Everyone and their plans."

Not only did Ory have to contend with the will of the River Road, but Millie thought he would have to abide by the will of God, someone Ory wasn't speaking to at the moment.

"I think God is going to have to get in line, Millie."

Ory walked away from her, looking up and down the columns and around the porch, examining, unnecessarily, lit candles, and flower arrangements around the door, fidgeting. "You know what, Millie? I do want to be happy here. But every good thing seems to come with a price."

Ory thought of Sidonie, and of his newly resurrected obligation, his love for her being the last of his family. Of Bernice, and a life lived in another time. But to Ory, as good as these things seemed, all brought with them parts of himself that he tried to kill. He continued, "I have yet to feel hope."

"Hope? Hope is a gift, child. And I think you've seen enough of those." She looked at the guns strapped to his chest. "Many people long for that feeling, as you are now.

Everywhere they're hoping for a change, for justice, for the lives of their loved ones. Ask yourself, are you going to be the one who sits around waiting for hope, or are you going to be the one who brings it?"

To Ory, Millie was sweet, one of the few warm memories he had, and one of the oldest. She spoke to him tonight like she did when he was a child, but unlike his early childhood, he no longer listened to the ignorant ramblings from a person of faith.

"Good night, Millie."

Ory left Millie on the porch, made his way down the stairs, and to the River Road.

Ory was glad he let Will go ahead of him. It was the first that time he had been alone since he arrived, and needless to say, he was overwhelmed. He listened to the rocks grinding beneath his feet, the crickets, and the wake in the river. A symphony of the night that can only be heard by one.

In the distance, Ory saw a small fire lit just off the side of the road. Some slave quarters were near to there, and it was most likely the slaves congregating, taking advantage of the only time that they could somewhat call their own. Ory decided that he would make his way toward them, and he wasn't sure why. As he got closer he could hear the sounds of music echoing along the road. Ory's curiosity grew and his pace increased for a couple of steps, then like water down his back, a cold chill shot through his spine, and like a lamed animal, his walk trickled to a hobble, and stopped. The burst of a flame drowned out the crickets and the wind's wake. Ory turned, and just off the road saw a dark figure puffing, drawing from the flame as smoke rolled out into the road.

"They sure do like to sing." Out of the shadows and into the moonlight, Lezin stepped out onto the road. That sense of fear and curiosity came to Ory, and he contemplated both running and sitting. Lezin looked out to the flames and music. "Have you ever listened to them?"

Ory wasn't sure how to respond, he was still focused on whether or not he was safe. Lezin was admiring, "One of the most beautiful sounds I've ever heard."

He replied cautiously, "I remember a little. From when I was a kid."

"Some say that there are secrets in those songs. That's a nice thought, huh? You know what I say to that? I say, let them be. People can't survive without it. You know what I mean?"

"I'm not sure I do."

"Hope. People need hope or they can't survive."

There was that word again. Hope.

"I say let them have their hope. It'll keep them alive until tomorrow. And for most, one day they'll wake up and find that tomorrow never came. And when they're old and dying they will wonder, Should I have been the one who died running? Because that's what hope breeds.

Those who wait, and those who run. Either way, hope keeps them alive. And me employed."

Lezin looked at the flames in a way Ory had never seen. A man's face contorting and shifting as if various images passed by him in the night. He saw anger, enjoyment, and frustration all roll over his face at once. Ory stood in his smoke that was now all around him. Lezin broke his focus on the flames and became slightly irritated, "You don't remember me, do you? I don't guess she spoke of me much."

Ory's mind began to churn, and he thought hard. He dug into his memory, trying to connect Lezin to his past, but unlike his other memories that tried to break free, this one hid and buried itself deep.

"Not many people will tell you. But we...we were friends."

"Good ones?"

Lezin snapped at Ory in a hiss, "Yes."

Ory's head pulled back a little, and upon that serpent-like action, something in his mind clicked. He recalled fights and arguments had in corners thought hidden and unheard.

"Your father never liked me coming around. He didn't like what we had."

He was right. Ory remembered his father and mother late in the night yelling over another man. Someone his father didn't want her to see. Just as his parents tried to hide those encounters from him, they continued today as memories hidden. But they couldn't hide then, and they wouldn't hide now. Upon remembering this, Ory became disappointed. This memory had lost its mystery, and he wanted nothing to do with the dealings of his parents and their old friends. He hoped for something more. Ory said, "I'm sorry to hear that."

"I tried to help her. To warn her."

"Warn her of what?"

"Of your father."

Ory turned to stone, he couldn't breath, paralyzed by the thought, and after a moment his breath shattered his frozen state. Lezin's dark eyes were on him as they reflected the distant flames. Ory wouldn't let his gaze hold him this time, and he continued down the road.

"Good night, sir."

"There's more, Ory. There's more I want to tell you."

"My parents are dead. Their old affairs are none of my concern."

"You need to know the truth, son."

Ory turned, snapped, also in a hiss, "I am not your son."

Though Ory was silhouetted by the flames down the road, the moon found a way to hit Ory's eyes through the darkness. Lezin looked upon a man who found light in the shadows, and as Ory turned and walked away, a feeling came over Lezin, one he had never felt before. He was afraid. And he smiled because he enjoyed it.

As Ory got closer to the music he noticed men and women sitting around the fire, all slaves. Johnny was there playing his guitar, strumming hard as a woman sang. Ory approached them, and when Johnny saw him he stopped playing. They all looked and stared at Ory. Something was different. Maybe it was the guns strapped at his sides, but it didn't feel like the River Road anymore. Their circle and bond didn't try to pull him in. And then it hit him. He wasn't welcome. Oddly, that made Ory feel more comfortable. He took a gracious step closer, easing them with, "Please. Don't stop."

The woman who was singing looked to Johnny, unsure of what to do. Johnny nodded to her, assuring her it was fine to play for him, but in the back of his mind he hoped that Ory liked what he heard, like in his dreams, and then he could play forever. Johnny took to his strings and the woman started to sing, as Ory leaned on one of the trees around them and listened. She sat calmly, gently rocking back and forth, her eyes closed from time to time as her deep voice shook the rocks along the River Road.

She sang about the winter and spring, of roads and rivers, the talk among the birds and the coming of the sun, following dead trees leading to valleys, valleys to canyons, canyons to home. She sang of that star, hanging in the sky like a jewel, whose light was worth more to her than any other she'd known.

The light from the center dwindled as a fire roared from inside the woman, among the flame and flicker of

Johnny's hands. Ory had never seen passion like that. The strumming continued and they transitioned into a hum, and so went this spiritual ritual. Ory could not help but to think, *Lezin was right.* It was one of the most beautiful sounds that he had ever heard. Ory, standing unwelcome, watched them all together in their few moments of harmony. And just beyond them, he saw the dark figure watching them as Ory did. Listening. He saw a burning eye floating across in the night, that ember's glow and fade, each time lighting his face just enough to catch that scar, until the eye vanished, and only smoke remained.

FOR REASONS UNKNOWN

The Bertran's home was on the River Road, not far from the sugar mill. From outside you could usually hear the arguing, the yelling, the slapping, all the sounds that come with a home run by a man mad at the world. Henri beat his children on occasion. Beat his wife more often. A man content with settling all his problems with violence, answering all his questions with it. Tonight was no different.

Henri and his wife had just come in from the party. She took his coat off as he plopped down at their kitchen table. He placed his bottle before him and with one eye gazed down the top. His wife saw this as she was hanging up his coat and rushed over to the counter to grab his jug of moonshine. Henri said, "That's okay, I'll get it."

She insisted, "Let me get it for you."

She tried so hard to be helpful, but she was so nervous. Accidents are bound to happen when someone's only purpose is trying not to have them. His wife grabbed the jug, and when she turned around to bring it to him, she lost her footing, falling to the ground taking the jug with her. It smashed and splattered on the ground. Henri didn't say anything at first, but his wife scrambled to retreat when the speed of his breath began to increase. Henri stood up against his will, walking to her as if ordered, thinking it was something he had to do.

"I told you, I'd get it." And he let it out as he slapped his wife across the face and yelled, "Don't. You. Listen?"

He grabbed his bottle and went to leave, his wife crying, "Don't you do it. You stay in this house."

And he walked through the door. He was always that way and no one would ever know why. Maybe it was because that's all he'd seen and never had another pair of eyes to show him otherwise. No one to help him step back and see himself for what he was.

Henri stumbled out of his home leaving the sounds of crying and yelling. He sipped the last drop out of his moonshine bottle and threw it to the ground and walked. He made his way to the sugar mill and to the slave quarters near it. Drunk. He approached the quarters and walked past the huts that the slaves slept in, looking for a certain one, struggling with his blurry vision to find the right door. When he did, he approached it and he did not open it or beat it down, he gently knocked. It slowly cracked open and there stood a young, beautiful, black slave. Her eyes were tired, woken from an ever-restless sleep.

"I am going to need some help in the mill."

The woman turned to the other women inside, all of whom had sorrow in their eyes, none wishing to be her right now, but all thinking, it was her turn to answer the door.

"Come on, let's go."

Henri softly pushed the door open and escorted her out of the hut and closed the door behind her.

The two entered the mill. Stacks of bundled cane were all around them. It was pretty clean and it didn't look like there was much work to be done. The woman said, as if she didn't know already, "So what would you have me do, sir?"

"Just come stand over here and help me with this."

She didn't refuse, not that she didn't want to, but she knew too well her options. Do what he wanted and go to sleep, or do what he wanted and go to sleep bruised. Once next to him she put her hands on one of the bundles, leaning against them. Henri came from behind her and rubbed his nose on the side of her face, slowly caressed up her arm with his fingers, kissed her neck, and all the while her face was flat and unmoving. Dead. Henri tried to be calm and gentle with her, like a man invited, imagining he was her lover. He placed his hands on her hips. He squeezed. Her eyes closed. Henri pressed his body against hers and reached to brace himself with his hand against the cane. But when his hand came down on it, it caught the end of a large sharp hook hanging from the cane, one used to help lift the bundles. Henri pulled away from her. Blood came pouring from his hand. The cut was deep. The woman turned to see the blood. She watched as fury formed before her, then that used feeling turned to horror, and she tried to subdue him.

"I'll get something for that."

Rage flashed into his eyes, and all that was calm and gentle in this moment had left him, and she felt the back of his hand across her face as she fell onto the cane. She screamed.

Henri tried to silence her. "Shut up."

He jumped on top of her and slapped her again. She screamed again, knowing this time it was different, she saw in his eyes that if he didn't stop, then it would be her heart that did. She tried to make a sound that those in the huts would not expect, one that wasn't usual, but they wouldn't discern it as anything different, and they'd sit and wait, not knowing she wouldn't return. He slapped. She screamed.

"Shut up, I said!"

Tired of her screams, Henri, his body pinning her to the floor, wrapped his fat, blistered hands around her neck and squeezed, then listened to the wail drop to squeak, as she choked for air.

Will was heading home along the road, and just as he passed the sugar mill he heard the scream. His normal instinct would be to stay out of trouble. If he had known why she was brought in there, and not of her current plight, he would have sat and listened like the others. But the woman inside the mill would be thankful for his mistake, as he ran, flying down the road to the mill, blasting inside.

Will came into the mill to see Henri trying to squeeze out what little life she had left. Will froze, hoping not to be seen by him. But Will also saw her eyes, and as she did before, he too saw her end if he were to do nothing. So, he breathed out, "Mr. Henri."

Henri turned to Will and let her go. The woman sucked in air and rolled off the cane, trying to crawl away. Henri slowly rose, examining Will, locking so intently on him that the woman managed to get up and escape out of the mill.

"What the hell are you doing here?"

Henri was in shock from the sight of Will. He wondered why he was out here this late. Why he was dressed in fine clothing.

"What are you doing in those clothes?" Henri grabbed Will's sleeve. He felt how smooth it was, smelled the sweet scent it acquired from the perfumes at the party. He slapped him in the face. "You steal these?"

"No, sir, I—"

Henri threw him against the cane, Will taking the place of the woman before. "Don't move."

"Please, sir. Master Ory—"

"Shut up, nigger."

Will was face first against the cane. Henri grabbed the collar of his shirt from behind and ripped it down over his shoulders. He walked over to a wall where tools for the mill were hanging and grabbed the reins used for horses. Walking back over to Will, "I'll teach you to steal from a white man."

Henri let the reins uncoil onto the ground, flung them behind him, then forward, lashing onto Will's back. And as the crack rang out, so did Will's screams.

"Please, sir. Please."

Whip. Will's heart pounded.

"Never trust a nigger. Never."

WHIP. Will was losing his grip on control.

"PLEASE."

Like the whip itself, Will cracked, no longer able to hold on, just as he did in the fights those days in the barn, and he turned to Henri just as he cocked back for another swing and pushed Henri clear across the room, slamming him into the piles of cane. Will snapped out of it, shaking his head, realizing what he'd just done. He dropped to the ground, lowering himself. "I'm sorry, sir."

Henri's face exploded as he let out a cry summoned by his rage. Will realized this just might be his end. He saw in Henri's eyes that inexplicable hatred. Will waited for the moment when Henri took that whip and tried to lash the life out of him. But that moment never came. Henri didn't move. He stood, still growling at Will, leaning against the wall of cane.

"Mr. Henri?"

Will looked closely as Henri's growls turned to gurgles and blood began to pour from his mouth. Will saw two spots of red revealing themselves through his shirt. Will ran over to Henri, who when he slammed into the stacks of cane, had fallen into two hooks that were hanging on its side, piercing him straight through his back. Will grabbed him and lowered him to the ground. The hooks were deep. He shook him.

"Mr. Henri."

What life Henri had left escaped him and Will cradled him in his arms as the blood slowly stopped pouring out, as his heart stopped pumping it. Will sat still, holding him, not knowing what thoughts he should have for this corpse, floating in the uncertainty of the impossible situation he now found himself in.

Ory was walking the same route home as Will when he heard the scream. Henri's. And just as a scream sent Will flying into the mill, so it did Ory. And in he came, flying through the door. When he saw Will holding Henri in his arms, sitting like marble, the world around Ory became still, and all he saw was a door at the end of a long hall. His body glided toward it, he reached for the brass knob, grabbed it and turned, pushing the door slowly open. It was a bedroom, with a small crib in the corner, and there, at the base of the bed, was Will holding Henri's bloody body. Will turned to him and Ory saw no regret, no remorse, but he also saw no misery or sympathy. Will held the bones of a man, completely bereft of feeling, shot beyond a moment that would force a man's humanity to a world of complete nothingness. Amidst this, Ory was overcome by the screams of a woman and the cries of a baby, and his world spinning around this image where Will could either be sinner or saint. Then the screams faded and the bedroom dissolved until all that was left was cane, blood, and silence.

"Will?"

Will did not break from his still world.

"Will, what happened?"

"I...I pushed him."

"Did you kill him?"

Looking for the answer himself, "Did I?"

Ory noticed the blood on Will's hands, on his shirt, saw Will's back and the gashes across it. He could have believed Will if he said it was an accident, but only if Ory did not have to see him in the state he was in now. Though everyone knew of the destructiveness that Henri delivered to the flesh, it wouldn't matter. Even if it looked like an accident, which it didn't. If caught, Will was going to hang. But none of these things were at the forefront of

Ory's mind. And none of those things were what caused him to do what he did next.

"Leave him."

Broken out of his stare with the dead, "Master Ory?"

"Will, get up." Ory grabbed him and lifted him to his feet. "We are going to run."

Will's eyes drifted back to the body.

"We stay off the road. We stop for nothing."

And as fast as they flew into the mill, they were out of it, running hard into the night, leaving Henri's lifeless body lying in a pool of his own blood, pierced in the back with the tool of a slave.

WITHOUT KNOWING WHY

By the time the sun rose the sugar mill was filled with men, no slaves tending to the cane, just law men and the Bertran boys. It was quiet among them as they stood over the cold, dead body. CJ was there, and his father, the sheriff. They remained calm and silent so as not to stir the Bertran boys, who were doing a good job not bursting into anger, given the situation. Jean paced back and forth waiting for the sheriff, who was kneeling down with CJ examining the body. The sheriff, looking to the hooks in Henri's back, "Looks like they pierced his lungs."

Jean's pace quickened as his agitation grew.

CJ concurred, "It probably didn't take long."

Jean stopped pacing and in his last attempt to stay civilized he stated, "How my father died is not as important as who killed him, Sheriff."

"We're getting to that, Jean."

He could hold on no longer, flinging himself toward the sheriff, wishing he could grab and shake him. "Obviously it's one of them niggers."

"Just calm down, son."

"Jacques, get me a rope. I am going to start hanging each one of these niggers until I find out who killed my paw."

"Your father had been drinking, this could have been an accident."

"Accident? Sheriff, there's blood spots leaving the barn."

The sheriff didn't think that it was an accident. He was just trying to do what he could to keep Jean from doing anything rash. But it didn't work. Jacques came back with a rope and looked for a secure spot to string it up in the mill.

"Now, if you are done insulting my intelligence, court is about to be in session."

Meeting Jean with similar aggression, "And when you're done hanging them all, what are you going to do then? What are you going to do when they're all dead and you still don't know who killed him?"

Jean realized his plan was impetuous and settled himself down, biting his bottom lip, not liking to appear foolish. "I just want justice, Sheriff."

Trying to ease him, "Then leave and let us do our job. Comfort your mother."

Begrudgingly the boys left the mill, leaving CJ and the sheriff to deal with the body of their late father. Jean didn't like being told what to do, nor did he like someone getting the better of him. But their bitter walk became a gift. For whatever reason, be it because of their inability to deal with their contempt for the sheriff or the fact that they were children who brought no comfort, they did not walk back to their mother in the house, and instead, they walked away from everything, avoiding the scene of death, away from the mill and the plantation, toward the solace of the trees, and there, just before the woods became thick, would be their prize. Jean spotted on the ground a red tie. One with the initials *O.L.F.* on it. Maybe it passed through Oak's mind as the right thing to do, to run back and show it to the sheriff. But it did not pass through his brothers' minds, and that is not what they did.

Ory and Will sat in a room in the front of his home, by windows where they could look outside for anyone approaching. Next to them was Will's bloody shirt and used gauze from treating his wounds. The Colts that Ory was given now hung on the back of a chair. Ory looked outside wondering if they were safe. Will looked at Ory and wondered the same. They began to hear the morning song of the house as it woke, the wood cracking as it felt the coming heat, the thud of footsteps, and the squeaking of doors. Will tried to figure, would Ory just let him go about as if nothing happened or would he turn him in? Grabbing the nearest blunt object and hitting Ory over the head with it never came to his mind, as it may have for most who felt the urge to run. But Will trusted Ory. He saw him in the same light as when Ory was an innocent child with a righteous heart, even if he now lacked those virtues. Besides, Ory had given Will no reason to believe he planned to turn him in, but still, he had planned nothing.

"Do we have a plan, Master Ory?"

"No."

He was still looking outside. Ory's stare was rooted and cold, like back in the library up North in his days of waiting. Will listened as the sounds of the house grew louder, as the people within it stirred.

"They're waking up, Master Ory."

"I know."

Will started fidgeting. That urge that escaped him earlier crept into his mind. While they sat there, waiting, people would enter, see them, see the bloody evidence, and it would all be over.

Growing impatient, "Master Ory—"

"Will, stop calling me that."

"Calling you what?"

"Just…"

Ory retreated back to the window. And as Ory turned away from what was inside, so would Will, both resigning to their submissive states. Will accepted it, letting go of his passion, again feeling that sense of binding and imprisonment, a world with no choice, a fate handed him at birth, and almost sacrificially said, "I'm going to die."

Will joined Ory, and as twin statues, they watched the sun rise into the sky, and as the light rose and its beams were cast on the two of them, a slow inhale brought Will's chest out, sitting him up straight, and starting as a rumble in his throat, Will let out a roar that stiffened the walls and ceased the morning song. As his yell faded back to a growl, Ory stayed next to him, never moving, until Will was silent, back gazing with him, looking outside, both sitting still.

Titaunt, in frantic concern, came running into the room, Sidonie right behind her, searching for who or what had made that sound. Seeing Ory, "Ory, what was that?"

"That was Will."

"Is everything okay?"

Neither of them responded. Titaunt, just as Will had suspected, noticed the bloody garment and the bandages just beside them.

"Ory?"

Still nothing. The two of them had no idea what they were going to do. Ory had thought all night about it. Part of him thought he could find a way to forget it all, just as Will had wondered earlier. But he knew there would be questions. Someone would have to pay, and if not Will, then someone else. All that mattered to Ory was that he had to keep Will alive, because somehow, in the whirlwind of all that had happened, Ory had found something that he couldn't yet explain, but he didn't want to lose it. Ory left the bloody garments out for Titaunt to see. He knew when this started it would all come rushing in and he needed her to know that this was not a game, and that this was the truth.

"Ory, why is there blood on this shirt?"

"There was an accident."

"Accident?"

"Calm down. Listen, all you need to know is there was an accident. But it is imperative that if anyone asks about me or Will, you saw us come home last night and we went to sleep." Turning to Sidonie, "Sugar, you were sleeping all night and you never saw these, okay?"

"I don't understand."

"This blood, it's not Will's blood, it's not mine. It's someone else's."

Ory threw the shirt to Will, and he knew then it was time to hide them, so Will stashed them away in one of the fine cabinets in the room.

"Now, they're going to be looking for whoever did this, but we can't tell them the truth because they'd never believe it."

"But who was it that—"

"Titaunt, trust me."

It happened sooner than he expected, and it was worse than he thought. While talking to Titaunt, they had taken their eyes off the window, and through the door came not the sheriff or the Bertrans, but Bernice.

"Ory. Oh, thank God. I was so worried."

Titaunt looking for answers, "Bernice, what is going on?"

"I'm assuming you haven't heard. Henri Bertran was killed last night and they don't know who did it. Since Ory had passed by there last night, I was worried something could have happened to him, too."

Titaunt slowly turned to Ory, searching his eyes, begging in her mind that it wasn't true. "Ory?"

Ory and Titaunt for a split moment appeared as mother and son. One looking for a reason not to be upset, the other overcome with the guilt of disappointing. Ory wondered if Titaunt thought he should have stayed up North. Bernice interjected, "What's wrong?"

It didn't take long for the silence to reveal to Bernice what had happened. And in a few moments she knew he was there. Ory knew what happened.

"My God. You didn't…"

"No, I didn't."

The entire energy in the room seemed to float to Will whose face was fighting a confessing look. Will avoided connecting eyes with any of them, which he thought would reveal the truth. Unfortunately, not looking at them did exactly that.

"Like I said before, it was an accident."

Titaunt, trying to put her foot down, "It doesn't matter. You have to tell them."

"No."

"Ory, they find out that Will did this and you hid him —"

"I am not turning him in."

Bernice jumped in, "What kind of an accident? They're saying he was murdered."

"Which is why no one in this room is going to say anything."

"Why are you doing this?"

"I don't…they hang him."

"Well, if he did it, isn't that what he deserves?"

"It wasn't his fault."

"Did you see it?"

"No."

"No? Then how do you know it was an accident?"

Ory knew he couldn't do it. He couldn't tell them the truth. Was he to tell them of his dream, of the long hall, and the brass knob? No. What he was doing was already crazy enough.

"This is ridiculous, Ory. Why risk your life on the word of a slave?"

Ory noticed Sidonie and her confused look. "I think it's best if Sidonie not be here for this."

Titaunt pulled her away and told her quietly, "Go upstairs and stay there until I come to get you, okay?"

Sidonie didn't realize the severity of the situation, nor did she find it necessary to leave, and it was that innocence that brought her to neglect their concern and focus on her own by saying, "Where's Ory's tie we made him? Do you think he didn't like it?"

As quiet as she may have sounded, Ory heard her. He looked to his chest, felt under his vest, checked his pockets, and ran around the room searching every corner he had been in that night, until he came to a stop, and froze. He slowly looked to everyone. Sidonie, Bernice, Titaunt. Maybe that was his somber way of saying it. And they all heard it. There was only one thing he could do now. Ory looked to Will, "We have to go."

Bernice went for him, "Ory—"

"Johnny," he yelled as he turned to Titaunt, "Listen, they'll be coming. When they get here, you never saw us. None of this. The blood, nothing, you hear?"

Johnny came running into the room.

"Johnny, bring two horses out to the back."

"Yes, sir."

"We'll head for the city. I'll figure things out there."

Bernice commanding him, "No, you won't."

"Nothing I tell them will matter. It's not fair to him."

"What about what's fair to me? You're willing to throw that away?"

Ory grabbed the Colts and draped himself with them as Bernice's words passed right through him.

"How do you know he's not lying to you?"

"I don't."

Ory fastened the holsters to his body tightly. Bernice's frustration with him sprung to anger. "You do this and it ruins everything. They'll call you a nigger lover. Ory!" At the peak of her rage, Ory finally looked to Bernice, who desperately continued, "Ory, you'll be the one who hangs."

He was willing to take that risk. He had to. And so he turned and made his way to the back door. Venom flew from Bernice's tongue in a bitter warning. "You do this and you're just like your father."

Ory's head whipped around, and coiled back as if to strike. "I am nothing like my father."

Bernice's facade faded away and all that was left was a tired girl, holding on to a dream promised to her long ago, one she thought of many nights in her plantation cell, and she begged, "He's a slave. His life is nothing compared to what we were promised. What fate has decided."

In that Ory saw Bernice truer than in any other moment he had been there. She held hard onto the only thing that had kept her going. Him. That realization would be the one that sealed his decision to flee, because he would hold on, too, hold hard to this change in him, this altering memory, or fall back into his frozen world, unable to change it again.

Sidonie, who had not found her way upstairs yet, was looking out the window, out to the road when she yelled, "Someone's coming."

Ory looked out to the road and saw the Bertran boys approaching. Titaunt grabbed Sidonie, Ory sat down behind a table in the middle of the room, Will right behind him, and Bernice stood nervously, trying not to fall as her knees began to shake. Just as they settled, the boys flew in without knocking, Oak hunching over to get through the doorway. Slowly approaching the family and Will, Jean looked at them standing stiff and tight. Ory hoped this would pass as a typical morning, nothing out of the ordinary. But the unexpected rush of this morning's chaos was too much for them to conceal, and their superficial smiles and positions were obvious enough that even these fools could tell.

"Morning. I'd appreciate it if you'd knock next time."

Jean, not hesitating to question, "Where were you last night?"

"At my engagement party. Weren't you there?"

"No, I wasn't."

"I'm sorry. I didn't make the guest list."

Jean pulled out his gun and aimed it at Ory.

"I'm guessing you haven't heard about my paw?"

Staying calm, "No, I have. And I am sorry. But you have no reason to come into my home and pull a gun on me in front of my family."

Jean pulled it from his pocket and threw it onto the table. Ory's tie. It fell as the judge's gavel. "You were there. You know what happened."

Ory was silent, he was always good at thinking on his feet, but nothing came to him. There was no good answer. Jean pulled the hammer back on the gun which caused Bernice to explode.

"Wait. Ory didn't do anything, it was Will. Don't kill him, it was—"

Titaunt grabbed Bernice who almost threw herself into the line of fire. "Get over here, are you crazy?"

Jean watched as Bernice settled down and then looked back to Ory. "That true?"

Jean's heartbeat quickened, his chest began to rise higher and higher with each breath.

"Listen, she doesn't know what she's talking about."

Jean bit that bottom lip of his and sneered at Will. "You kill my paw?"

"Jean, look at me. Look at me. You don't want to do this."

"Oh, yes I do."

Jean never looked to Ory again. It is in moments like these, in those split seconds where time freezes, when most people fail to do anything, but some, they act without control, their mind steps aside and lets something else take over for a short period of time, something that lives deep inside them. And so it happened to Ory as he flipped the table up, knocking the gun out of Jean's hand and kicking him into his bothers, knocking them all off balance, while Ory and Will were out of the house, scored by the screams of their loved ones.

Sure enough, as they broke out of the back, the horses that Johnny had prepared for them were there, waiting for their riders.

"Get on the horse."

Ory jumped onto the horse from behind, springing into the saddle. Will approached the side of his steed, trying to get his foot into the stirrup. "I can't."

"Just mount him."

Ory rode up next to him, grabbed Will, helping him into the saddle, guiding his horse next to his own, and they rode off. The Bertrans came out of the home firing a few shots, running around to the front of the house for their horses, only to find them gone. Then inside the home, Johnny was looking out to see Ory flying down the road, smiling at his success in getting rid of the Bertrans' horses, knowing no one would follow his master and friend.

The three ladies came out of the home once the danger was clear. They looked down the empty road watching the dust slowly settling back down to the ground. They stood, pondering the terrors that would be after Ory and Will, frightened of the possibilities if they were to return.

Ory and Will rode off together along the River Road until they came to a new one, and there they turned, taking a different route toward a new destiny. They could feel the River Road trying to rope them in and pull them back, even as it lay behind them. Will's mind had broken open to a new world he'd inevitably see, but he could think of none of it. It was filled instead with the different hounds that would be after him. And in Ory's mind, there were only two things that consumed him. The churning of a desperate memory...and the man of shadow and scar. They blazed through their fears and out of their prisons, out of the hands of the River Road and embraced the horror of this new one, a road where every choice that they made from there on out would solely be their own.

RELEASING THE HOUNDS

Given how Ory was begged to come home, how he was treated upon arrival, you'd think that they'd find it hard to believe, that there must have been some mistake, but not many did, and most accepted it quite quickly. The plantation's porch had now become a congregation of men, Cogan and those who would be after Ory and Will. The sheriff and CJ, the Bertran boys, a man from the city newspaper, and Lezin, whose men were in the group listening while he stood apart, down the porch, smoking. Cogan was on his feet, standing behind his empty rocker, giving orders to the man from the newspaper, repeating himself over and over, each time with more passion. "Now remember, time is important."

"Sir, we are going to move as fast as we can."

"I want you to move faster than that. I want everyone in the state to have seen their picture and know they're out there."

"But sir—"

"Just print their damn faces." Trying to control himself, "have it done tomorrow, or you might as well resign."

Cogan sat in his rocker. He had been going on for some time. He rocked back catching his breath, looking out to the mighty river in front of him, seeing all the things he had lined up, his plans slowly washing away.

"What am I going to do now?"

The men said nothing. They all knew how much he had invested in Ory, and Cogan's conversation with the man from the newspaper had been less than benevolent. They would have stood in silence, until given an order or asked a question, but they wouldn't wait long as Bernice walked in. Cogan dropped his distraught appearance in exchange for a compassionate one and said, "Bernice? How are you feeling?"

"Any news?"

"No, but our friend from the paper is going to help us get some soon."

The man gave Bernice a smile.

"He's going to make sure our boys have nowhere to go. Don't worry. We'll catch him."

"He's not going to be hurt, right?"

What pain that Ory could receive had not crossed Cogan's mind. There was only the River Road, what he owed it, what Ory owed it, everything that had been set in place for his daughter and his own lineage. No, he didn't think of Ory's pain. Not yet.

"Right. He'll be fine."

It became obvious that the men around had been waiting a while and were ready to hear what Cogan had to say to them. Upon Cogan seeing this, and wanting to remove himself from this talk with Bernice, he said, "Bernice, could you please return to the house? I'll let you know when we're done."

"If it concerns my future husband, then it concerns me."

Not one man looked at Cogan when she said that. Ory was the accomplice in a murder, if not a murderer himself, and on the run with a slave, and Bernice was still considering him. The men kept their eyes down, but in the distance, Lezin stood laughing. Cogan let her be, rocked in his rocker, and then let the men speak. "Go ahead, Sheriff."

"What we are dealing with isn't just a slave on the run, these are murderers. I suggest you let the marshal take care of this."

Jean tried to refute, "If you think we're just going to sit here and wait around—"

"Not many men on this porch would appreciate you speaking right now, Jean."

Everyone leered at the Bertran boys. If not for them, everyone on the porch would be sitting in judgement with Ory in front of them.

"What?"

"You've done enough already."

"You think I'm not going after the bastards that killed my paw?"

The sheriff went back to Cogan, not answering Jean, knowing for sure that he wouldn't listen. He knew because the sheriff wouldn't have taken his own advice in that situation either.

"It's best you leave this to the marshal, Mr. Lasseigne."

Cogan continued his rocking, looking out to the river. He was listening. "I thought him being up North would have helped him."

It was Cogan's idea to send Ory North. He thought it would've helped him deal with the loss of his mother if he didn't have to be around this place all the time, reminded of her everywhere he went. He'd finish school, further his studies and return home when he was ready, and by then, maybe it would've made him forget. Not about his mother, but about something else. Cogan agreed, "You're probably right."

"It won't be safe sending everyone after him. More are going to get hurt."

"Father, that is absurd."

"Bernice—"

"Ory is not dangerous."

"At this point, signs suggest that they were in this together. A man with his condition—"

"Condition?"

"A man in his situation—"

"Situation? What, running in fear because no one will listen to him? He said it was an accident."

"Accidents don't happen like this. And it makes it harder to believe when it involves someone like Ory."

"That is not him."

The pressure between them was building. One learning to speak for herself, the other craving to shut her up.

From down the porch a voice broke them up. "You can all stop dancing around it."

Lezin was still out at the end of the porch, looking back as they all looked at him dumbfounded by his words. He continued, "You're all thinking it."

Everyone slowly looked to one another, seeing if the other was going to be the one who said it. Except for the newspaper man, who was from the city. He was lost in all this and said, "Thinking what?"

The sheriff, thinking that maybe it was his responsibility, tried to break the awkwardness, but perhaps made it more so by saying, "Ory has a...a family history. Involving violence."

Then Cogan thought they all, including himself, were being timid. Mostly because no one ever wanted to believe it. And if they never said it out loud, maybe it didn't actually happen. But it did.

"His father was a murderer. Not many years before we sent Ory up North for school, he killed Ory's mother. He tried to make it look like a suicide, but was caught."

From the day Ory had left until then, this was seldom said, and when it was, it was quiet and in dark corners. Most didn't say it at all. They were quiet now, but Bernice would still not let it go. "A fact that is irrelevant in this matter."

Cogan slowly stood from his rocker. He looked to the river again, as if it was telling him what he should do, and said, "No one goes. Leave it to the marshal."

Jean stormed off the porch, bumping CJ in the shoulder as he left, his brothers right behind him, bitter from the decision Cogan had made.

"We'll be here, sir, if you need us."

The sheriff and CJ left as well, the newspaper man with them. Lezin's men lingered for a moment, and then looked to Lezin who signaled that they could leave. All that remained were Cogan and Bernice and the river. They both looked to it.

"Do you think he did it?"

"It doesn't matter what I think."

"Father…"

Cogan did not to like her tone, but he tried to hold back his anger. "Why would he run, Bernice? He's either a murderer, a nigger lover, or both. Either way, it doesn't look good."

112

"His father being a murderer does not make Ory one."

"Something like that can really rattle somebody, not to mention Ory was very young when it happened. There's no telling the effect it could have had on him."

"We've all seen bad things. Ory is no different. This is just a misunderstanding."

"Girl, were you there?"

"I think—"

"WERE YOU THERE?"

"No, sir."

"Well, I was."

"I realize that, father, but—"

"Oh, do you? You know that Ory's father murdered his mother?"

Bernice became frightened by her father's overwhelming presence that was slowly approaching her, growing above her.

"Everyone knows."

"But do you, and everyone, know that Ory watched it happen? That he was the one who caught him?"

That part was only a rumor, and a rumor that not many told. Only a few knew. Titaunt knew. Millie knew. Not Bernice. She had become taken by the river, trying hard to see that boy lit on the horizon in her dreams, but it was beginning to fade, as if the two could not exist there together.

Cogan left Bernice alone. He walked to the other end of the porch to Lezin. He stood next to him. As strange as it may sound, Lezin would be the one he was most honest with.

"This is my fault. I tried too hard to make everyone believe things would be okay. And at some point that must have blinded me as I began to believe it myself. I thought that he could be my son."

Lezin looked to Cogan, aggravated by his statement. He said to himself, "He is not your son."

"What?"

"Nothing." Lezin wouldn't let it get to him. Instead he enjoyed watching as Cogan drifted away on a river of failure.

"Maybe you were right. Maybe this wasn't supposed to happen. The River Road will survive without him. He'll have nothing to do with my daughter."

Cogan found himself a new sense of drive rooted in protection. Protection of his daughter and his home, as a servant to the River Road.

"The sheriff thinks I should let the marshal handle this. I'm sure you know what I think about that. Whatever it takes, Lezin. Don't let them bring him back here. Unless it be to bury him."

He turned to leave, made a few steps toward the inside of the plantation and stopped, looking back over his shoulder to Lezin. "To look so much like his mother, and be ruled by his father."

114

Not long after that, Cogan was back in the planation. Lezin would stay there for awhile, thinking of his new assignment. His dream assignment. The finishing piece to his puzzle. You see, Ory was not the only one with a past. He was not the only one hiding. The River Road held many secrets and many nightmares. Most stood alone. But some were connected, intertwined in memories and linked over years of time, waiting for the right piece to come along, the key that would unlock the past. Ory didn't know it yet, but they were connected by more than just this chase. A connection Lezin would call family.

Not far from there another man was preparing for a journey, though he would not be chasing after Ory and Will. Back at Ory's home, Johnny was there to see everyone focus all their attention on the fugitives that had fled. Work had come to a stop and not much notice was paid to the slaves that day, which is what got Johnny thinking. *Why not?* he thought.

Johnny had packed a small bag and strapped his guitar to his back. He planned to run behind Ory and Will, but not right behind them. He'd wait for all those after them to pass, then he'd sneak into the dust they left behind. He thought they'd be so busy looking forward, they'd never bother to look back.

He did just that, falling in behind the hooves that galloped along the River Road, sneaking about in the places they had passed, and no one knew he left. They would get ahead of him eventually, and then he would be on his own, not knowing which way they had gone, hoping that the routes he would then blindly choose didn't bring them together again.

ONE MAN'S TRASH, ANOTHER MAN'S TREASURE

Ory and Will were walking their horses, they had been riding for hours. Well, Ory rode and Will hung on. He'd have bruises for the next few days from the abuse he had endured on the road. Will walked rubbing his neck, his ribs, his butt, trying to ease the pain.

"You're going to have to learn how to ride one of those."

"Yes, sir."

Will and Ory came to an old home set back on the edge of the swamp. Leaves filled the porch and trash was scattered all around the outside, the front door swinging open and closed in the wind.

"But we'll have to do it another day."

Ory slapped his horse sending it off down the road.

"What are we doing?"

"We need to get off the roads. Word is going to run up the river faster than we can."

"Then where do we go?"

Ory noticed a flat-bottomed boat lying on top of a stack of firewood.

"See that pirogue over there?"

"Yes."

"We're going to borrow it."

"But sir, if they catch us—"

Ory slapped Will's horse and it, too, flew down the road.

"Will, did you look at that house? No one has been there for years."

Ory didn't mind taking an abandoned boat. The ones who lived there obviously didn't want it, or else they would have taken it when they left. Once the two were standing above the boat, they started to pick it up when there was a gunshot. Chips of wood flew into the air. The two ducked behind the stack.

"What the hell is going on?"

"You God damn sons of bitches. I'll teach you to come on my property and steal my boat."

Ory was wrong, to say the least. On the trash filled porch stood a grizzled man, barefooted, and holding a rifle. He took aim and blasted more chips off of the wood above the two.

"I guess someone does live there, Ory."

"I can see that, Will."

Chips flew off of a log.

"You all come out so I can make this quick."

Will shocked Ory as he unexpectedly stood and yelled back to the owner, "Sir, we meant no wrong. We were just going to borrow it."

A bullet flew by Will as the owner fired off another shot. Ory yanked him back down behind the wood. "Stay down, damn it."

Ory was thinking hard. He looked down at the two Colts on his vest. He pulled one of them out holding it in front of his face. Instantaneously, images flashed, blinding his present sight. His mother's gravestone appeared to him, *Ory*, he heard screaming in his head. Next came Will holding Henri, bloody, back in the bedroom of his home. The gun was shaking. Then a soft deep voice found its way through the black wall deep within him and said, *It's okay, son. Just take a deep breath and hold it. Now, let it all go...and squeeze.*

"Ory."

Will yelled at him just as another bullet hit right near Ory's head. He looked to Will and could hear the owner reloading. He holstered his gun and grabbed one end of the boat. "Come on, Will. Move."

They picked the boat up and ran for the swamp. They threw the boat in the water as bullets plunged in along side of them. They jumped in, lying down to escape any more shots as they floated away, showered by the bullets splashing around them.

Will and Ory paddled through a vast thickness of duckweed. A jungle of cypress trees and moss surrounded them at every turn and with each stroke of their paddle, they went deeper into nowhere.

"Have you been out this far, Ory?"

"No."

"So, you don't think they'll find us here?"

"You're more alone right now than you'll ever be. The only thing is, we can't stay here forever."

They were off the road and in the swamp. It wouldn't take long for those who were after them to find their abandoned horses, and ultimately know where they were now. But on a boat like this, it would be nearly impossible to track them. But, they knew exactly as Ory did. Those two would eventually have to come out. So all they had to do was wait.

SINS OF THE SISTER

Titaunt sat, anxiously embroidering. Ory and Will were far from out of her thoughts. She was stitching her way through the night to distract herself from her inability to sleep. When her sister died, Ory and Sidonie fell under her care, and though Ory had been away for a long time, and was now a grown man, she would still hold her post.

Her attention was drawn to the front door. A creak came from behind it. *Or did it?* she thought. Uncertain if there had been a sound, she listened for another one. She felt a presence from outside. Looking upon the door, she could feel it about to burst open, shards of wood exploding in the air as the lock ripped through its frame. But it never happened. She stood, slowly making her way to the door. She stopped as she heard another sound, a creak on the porch from someone standing right outside, shifting their weight. Then silence. She began to walk again, getting closer to the door, she reached out for the knob, and just as she grabbed it, she pushed her body against the door, locking the lock. Her forehead pressed on the door as she continued to listen. There was no creak. Titaunt lifted her head off of the door, turning her ear to it, then from inside the house, she heard a small burst. Right next to where she was sitting was a man with fire in his hand, kneeling in the shadows next to the fireplace, lighting the wood inside. The shadow said, "The cold is coming."

Lezin threw the match into the fire and Titaunt didn't move from the locked door.

"Got to get this place nice and warm."

"What are you doing here?"

Lezin sat down by the fire, holding his hand out to the flames, the pops and crackles sent small embers up into the air, landing on and floating up around his palm.

"I had blocked her out of my mind, but him coming back here just stirred things up again."

Titaunt tried to control her breathing so as not to appear frightened, though that is what she was feeling in every finger, every muscle, feeling vulnerable in all the places where skin was exposed. Her face. Her neck. Her wrist.

"All that boy's face reminds me of is that bastard who took everything away from me."

"She never loved you."

"You really believe that, don't you?"

Lezin smiled, but a smile that covered the grinding of his teeth and he slightly laughed to mask his impulse to grab her. His dark eyes landed on Titaunt.

"What did he say when he left?"

"Nothing."

"No mention of what he might do?"

"I don't know anything."

Continuing his smile, he noticed the silver necklace around Titaunt's neck. Lezin stood admiring it, and as he floated across the dark room to her, he said, "Familiar. This yours?"

Titaunt pressed her back to the door as Lezin placed his arm against it, leaning in to get a closer look at the jewel. He ran his finger along the chain, down her neck and to her chest, fingering the silver leaves.

"When did you start wearing this?"

Standing her ground, and proud, "The day she died."

Lezin looked into her eyes, slowly becoming intoxicated by them. He could see her face in Titaunt's. They looked so similar.

"You look beautiful in it."

He slowly brought both hands up to her neck, slid them along it as if he were to choke her, but didn't. He just caressed her neck until his hands were behind it and he detached the necklace. "How about I hold on to this. Something to remember her by."

This new image of the woman before him swirled in his head and an infatuation found its way inside his dark mind, planting itself, and growing with each second he lay eyes on her.

"No," he said. "Something to remember you by."

Titaunt was starting to fail at hiding that fear that she had masked so well. Lezin put the necklace around his own neck and brought his hands to her face, ran his fingers up the back of her head through her hair. He placed his nose on the top of her head and took a deep breath. Lezin brought his lips to Titaunt's ear and whispered, "How about I give you something to remember me by."

He pulled her face towards his in pursuit of a kiss, which she resisted, which made him pull harder. She brought her hands to his chest, struggling to push him away, trying to turn her face, but his body kept getting closer and just before their lips met, the door to the room flew open.

"Get off of her."

Sidonie was standing in the room holding Ory's rifle, aiming it right at Lezin.

"Let her go, now."

Lezin let go of Titaunt and turned to Sidonie, holding his hands up in an easeful fashion, speaking softly, "Wait a second, little girl. Everything is okay."

He lowered himself to her level. "I'm not here to hurt anyone." His innocent look was starting to subdue Sidonie's attack as Lezin moved across the floor toward her. "Why don't you give me the gun and go sit by the fire. I made it nice and warm for you."

Lezin gently reached out for the gun, he would have grabbed it, too, if Sidonie had not caught another glimpse of Titaunt's terrified eyes, because when she did, all that was innocent about him disappeared and a bullet flew passed his head shattering a bottle on the table behind him. Lezin brought his hands back up and walked back with caution, smiling and laughing. "Okay, okay, I'm going."

Lezin was impressed with the fire in Sidonie. He turned and grabbed the knob from behind Titaunt, who moved to the side as the door opened.

"I'll find him. When I do, maybe I'll come back."

Standing in the doorway he looked down at Sidonie, still holding aim on Lezin and then over to Titaunt, taking in that invigorating sense she gave him.

"What a wonderful family."

The door remained open and he vanished into the night. Sidonie ran to Titaunt, dropping the gun, and collapsing in her arms crying. The two women sat on the cold wood floor in terror. Titaunt held her tight, applying pressure to a wound, a sight that would scar her forever. Sidonie didn't need this in her life, she didn't know about her mother yet, and one day she inevitably would, along with all the other truths about her family. Titaunt promised that she would be there to see her through it. And as she rocked her crying child, her eyes lay on the fire across the room, a blaze burning from the center of her home. The fire had Titaunt locked on its raging flames, as if Lezin's eyes still lingered in the room, and her fear for Ory grew. Her old concern for what the law would do to him was nothing compared to this, to the thing that would attack him from the inside, something after him that lived in his past, reborn upon his return.

TESTING THE SWAMP WATERS

Ory's body was shaking. The cold ground sent shivers through him as he slept. Will sat close to the fire they had made, trying to stay warm as the temperature dropped with the night air. Ory's shaking increased and Will became concerned, so he reached down, seeing if he could wake him. "Master Ory?"

Ory woke from his dream and into the chill of the night. It took him a moment before he realized where he was. At first he thought he was waking in his room back up North by the way he felt the cold in his lungs.

"You okay, sir?"

"Yes. Just cold."

"At least the mosquitoes aren't out."

They both huddled close to their small fire, listening to the sounds of the different creatures hidden in the swamp. They were used to it and could identify most of them. Frogs, coyotes, fruit bats. The noises they made were just louder than they were used to.

"Different here."

"Yeah."

"How much longer do you think we'll need to stay?"

"Not long."

Time went by and they sat in silence, one they both seemed to enjoy. Will grew curious about Ory and his dreams, his shakes, and all the rushes that came over him in the graveyard, with the Bertran boys, and earlier with the man protecting his boat.

"Ory?"

"Yeah."

"Back when we were being shot at, why didn't you shoot back?"

"I wanted to."

"But you didn't."

"Couldn't."

"That wasn't always the case."

"No, but it's not something I care to remember."

"I heard you were good with them."

"It was something my father and I used to do. Before he died."

Will remembered Ory's father from when he was a child. There were not many things that he could remember about him, and usually that was a sign to him that he was a good man. He remembered the guns. Seeing Ory and his father shooting. He didn't recall violence as most people did. If Will believed anything, it was in the things he could see.

"I remember your father. I think people are wrong about him."

Ory looked to Will, aghast by the comment, but so much so that he could only laugh.

"What's so funny, sir?"

"Will, you know how my father died?"

"Yes, sir."

The laughter was slowly slipping away, "And you don't find that statement absurd?"

"No, sir. I mean, what I remember of your father, he seemed alright...for a white man."

Ory did well in holding back his bitterness from Will's assumption. Will could feel that he may have gone too far and perhaps was taking too many liberties, but as tense as it had become, he found enjoyment in this interaction he had never had before, and he couldn't resist. "Millie says you were there when it happened."

For Ory it was similar. It was getting frustrating for him, but he, too, was thriving on their conversation and this may have been the only time Ory had ever talked about it. They found it easy to talk to each other despite the harsh realities.

"I was."

"Do you remember it?"

His question was perfect and all together ironic. The one question that no one would ever have asked Ory, was the one question that would get him to talk about it.

"It has played in my mind for as long as I can remember. Since the day it happened. It would come and go while I was away. Since I came back, I have no control, it takes over my mind, repeating itself no matter how hard I fight it."

As he spoke, he saw the dream that repeated. The one never-changing vision that roamed freely in his mind.

"Sidonie was just a baby. I came home to the sounds of screaming in my parents' bedroom."

He saw that long hallway and that door at the end. Screams as he approached it. He opened the door and there was Ory's mother lying across his father's legs. His parents were covered in blood. His mother's wrists were sliced. His father was holding a knife. He looked up to Ory. His face was plain, washed over without a care.

"She just lay there in his arms. He didn't do anything. I yelled and I screamed, but she didn't answer."

Ory was holding his hands out for his mother but her lifeless body didn't reach back. Instead he was pulled away from her, dragged back down the hall as she faded away. *Mama*, he cried.

"I didn't know what to do, I just took Sidonie, who was screaming in her crib, and ran for help. My father never said a word. They didn't even have a trial. He was dragged out into the middle of the town. I was there. His hands bound behind him." Ory leaned in toward Will. He had a little smile on his face, as if he were telling Will a joke and was about to hit the punchline. "And you know what he does? He knelt down before me and said, 'Learn to let it go, son. You must learn to let it go.' Then a few men pulled him away. I didn't know where they were taking him, until they stopped under a tree. He never struggled. Even as they tightened it around his neck. And I watched him hang."

Ory relaxed back in front of the fire. The flames caught his eyes and his artificial smile left him. Will wondered if he saw his father in those flames. And for that moment Will saw a truth in him. From the fire, Ory said, "It's insane, huh? My father murdered my mother, and he tells me to 'let it go.'"

Will thought about it. Maybe that was his mistake. He spoke to Ory honestly, from the enjoyment of their conversation. Maybe he should have just said what Ory wanted to hear. But Will didn't. And wouldn't take it back.

"Well, maybe you should."

Turning from the flames, "What did you say?"

"I said, maybe you should let it go."

The look that came over Ory was ineffable. The closest thing to having been betrayed, rage, sorrow, a need to grab Will and bury him in the fire, a need to run and never stop. Whatever that is, that's what it was.

"You listen to me real close. My choice to humor your questions was not to seek your advice. You understand me?"

"Yes."

"Yes, what?"

"Yes, sir."

Ory's possession was slowly pushed back down, reinforcing that black wall, and he returned to his barricaded self, trying to function calmly, as bitterness oozed from his pores.

"I'm sorry. I know you're trying to help. But my mother was taken from me, Will. And he took her. But I can't expect you to understand that. You don't know what it's like having something taken from you."

"I don't?"

They didn't speak again for the rest of the night. Neither had reason. Both angry at the other, and sympathetic as well, both guilty of their own ignorance. The fire would be all they looked upon until they fell asleep. But the alluring and most dangerous thing of all, was that as the two sat before each other, Will was never once shocked by the passion that took over Ory. Will didn't blink, because he had seen it before in himself.

MASTER AND SLAVE

They had put out their fire, traveled east out of the swamp, sunk the boat, all adding up to a half day's work, all done without a word. As Ory said, they would have to eat, and the longer they stayed in the swamp the dirtier they'd become, and less likely to pass others without suspicion. Once they were getting close to the town they finally spoke.

"Okay. We go in there, you're my slave. Alright?"

Ory was sure that he understood. The evening they had gone through wasn't one they'd like to relive, especially not when leading into a day like today. They were both sorry, but not terribly apologetic.

"If we don't appear that way, we will stand out and —"

"Yes, sir."

Both frustrated by each other's stubbornness, they walked into a small town. People were outside, walking

133

the street, going to markets and shops, banks and cafes. Some people gave a double take to Ory and Will casually strolling along the road. Will followed close behind Ory, hunched with his head slightly lowered, while Ory's chest was high and he walked with entitlement.

"Just stay behind me."

"I'm thinking this is a bad idea."

"Me, too. But we need to eat."

In the town was a sheriff's station. Inside and around it things were pretty sparse and bare. Behind a desk sat a short plump man looking into a mirror. He was a dirty little man, most of his clothes looked like they had been worn for years and washed rarely. But as he looked at his reflection, he was carefully positioning his new hat, clean, without a blemish. He'd baby that hat for as long as he could. His lawmen sat about the station, all wearing guns and badges, watching their boss finish looking at himself. The plump man, the Hatter, leaned back in his chair picking up a wanted poster.

"Looks like we got ourselves one of those abolitionists on the run with a nigger. Turns out, these two actually murdered a man. They're offering a reward for their capture. It'd be great to come across them. I could get this big boy some exercise."

The sheriff grabbed his crotch, thinking about how long it had been since his last time. He laughed obnoxiously, informing the other men, necessarily so, that he was telling a joke, to which they responded with laughter.

"This frog needs a basket."

His men looked at each other, unsure of what he meant, but laughed anyway, knowing that's what he expected.

Through the window of the station you could see Ory and Will enter a small restaurant as the Hatter threw the poster on his desk.

When they entered, there weren't many customers. It was mostly empty tables with only a few individuals eating alone in silence. But what few people there were, they all looked at Ory and Will as they walked in.

The owner of the establishment approached them immediately. "Good morning, sir."

"Morning."

"He can't eat in here."

"Well, I should hope not."

One of the customers there looked up at them from his food.

Ory continued, "I was going to have him sit on the floor by the door."

"It'd be better if he waited outside."

"Whatever you prefer."

And as if it came out of his mouth a thousand times, Ory said to Will, "Hey, nigger. Outside."

Will didn't move right away, he hesitated, and that wasn't fast enough to sell their story, so Ory kicked Will, speeding him up. "Go on."

Will shot up and scurried out of the restaurant, sitting just outside.

"Sorry, he can be stubborn sometimes."

The other customer who had become suspicious had soon forgotten about them, satisfied with Ory's handling of Will.

Ory sat down at a table and the owner brought him food. He didn't hesitate, being a hair short of ravenous. Stuffing his face, he could see Will outside through the window. He looked outside to his accomplice sitting, knowing Will was as hungry as he was.

Ory and Will had a similar problem, believing they were actually alone on this journey. To them, life was set, and as companions, they'd never understand the other. But this new road that they were on would change that. There was no telling what life had in store. And in this new realm, only one thing was true. They were both equal. They were partners. It didn't matter anymore who the other was. Those who hunted them saw only reward and revenge. They knew how each other felt because they felt the same, especially now, with the simple feeling of hunger. Ory got up with his plate in his hand, walked outside, stood over Will for a second and threw what was left on his plate down to him and it landed on the ground.

Just as fast as he did that, he walked back inside, handing the empty plate back to the owner.

"Thank you, sir. The bill?"

As the owner turned to retrieve it, a man who had been drinking came through the door. "Whose nigger is that outside?"

The owner turned, saw the man who had burst in, and instantly closed his eyes and took a breath, preparing for the man he'd seen often, and wished he didn't.

"Someone better move him, before I move him."

"He's mine. Don't worry, I was just leaving."

The drunkard walked next to Ory, looking him up and down, admiring the fact that Ory probably had money to spare, being that he had his own personal slave waiting for him outside.

"You think it pleases my appetite to see him outside?"

"No, sir. That's why I am leaving. Just give me a second to pay my bill."

"Well, the damage is done. I don't want to eat now. How are we going to fix that?"

Trying to satisfy him, "If you'll do me the pleasure, sir, I'd like to buy your meal."

"Sounds good. Do you hear that, Jeffery? This man's buying me lunch."

"I told you my name's not Jeffery."

"Well, whatever the hell your name is, get me my food."

Ory saw the frustration in the owner's eyes. He probably had to deal with this day in and day out.

"I don't know why I eat the crap here, anyway."

As Ory paid the bill, the man became intrigued by Ory for another reason.

"Do I know you?"

The drunkard looked through the window to Will, calculating something in his head. He leaned in a little to get a better look at Ory's face, but Ory didn't let him and he moved his face down to the bill.

"That's your nigger out there, right?" Raising his hand to turn Ory's face, "You look—"

Ory grabbed the man's hand from his face with one hand and with the other, the back of his head, smashing his face on the counter. Ory turned to the owner, "Is he bothering you?"

The owner almost fell back in astonishment, a huge smile on his face, as if he had done it himself. "Yes, sir."

Ory grabbed the gentleman by the the collar and dragged him through the door and threw him out, his body falling and rolling into the dirty street. The drunkard stumbled to his feet and scurried off. Will saw Ory standing in the doorway. Soon they would discover that the expected thing to do, wasn't always the best thing to do.

WHEN ALL THAT IS LEFT IS THE TRUTH

Thunder rolled as a storm lingered just beyond the river, creeping with its dark clouds along the water, following Bernice until she turned off the River Road and headed toward Ory's home. She could see it not far off, and as she was approaching, she ran into Millie who was taking linens down from a clothesline, startling her.

"Good evening, ma'am."

"Millie. You scared me."

"Sorry, ma'am."

Lightning lit up the sky and distant thunder rolled.

"I hope it stays away."

"I don't. Great things can be born out of a storm."

"You think?"

"Yes, ma'am. Ory and Will were born inside one."

"They were born on the same day?"

"Indeed. Almost the same time, too. Boy, those babies cried. Just about made me crazy, I tell you. I felt for them, though. Coming into this world amidst a flash and a rumble. But then," preparing Bernice for her favorite part, "light was shining on Ory's face and when we looked to the sky, the sun peaked out through the clouds. Ory just stopped. Not a sound. But little Will just kept at it. Just roaring at the sky, trying to scare those clouds away."

Bernice smiled. She enjoyed hearing this story of the past. It took her mind off of the present. And to hear Millie tell it was soothing to her, pacifying the anxiousness that had been building.

Millie went on, "They were the light and the lion. Both the same, though, if you ask me. The same person just living two different lives. That's what is going to keep them alive, their strength together."

Bernice didn't take well to the finishing of the story, having to come back to the world of life and death. She had been thinking lately of the decisions she had made and wondered why she made them.

She confided in Millie, "The day Ory left, I tried to give Will away. I didn't think about what I was doing at the time. I didn't care that he was going to die. The thought never crossed my mind. All I could think about was Ory."

Millie thought about Bernice's love for Ory, and how that could cloud someone's judgement. But she was not at all blind to the fact that Bernice saw Will's life as having less value compared to Ory's.

"That was a hard situation."

Bernice waited for Millie to say more, but she didn't. Feeling a slight tension, Bernice agreed. "Yes."

Millie continued to unhang the sheets and fold them, looking at Bernice, waiting for her to continue because she could tell there was something she wanted to say. Millie knew well, there are times in people's lives when realizations are made, where light shines on the darkness around them. And when it happened to Bernice, like most, she never thought about what it meant to others or the pain it brought them. She was young and eager and naive, but Millie chose not to harbor anger towards her, and instead chose to see this as her beginning. As Bernice continued, Millie would endure.

"How do you do it?"

"Do what?"

"Do you...do you hate us?"

"There's enough hate on this road to last another hundred years and more. It doesn't need any from me."

"How can you always be so happy?"

"What if I told you that the ones who lived with the most horror and hate, seemed like the happiest ones of all?"

Millie smiled and she continued her folding. Bernice was speechless for the moment, unsure of the level of Millie's seriousness. But it was what she wanted to hear. It helped set in place this new feeling that Bernice could not yet describe.

"As I step away from myself, what I thought was bright and pristine is fading. I fear what's behind it."

"The River Road blinds you to many things, Bernice."

"What?"

"It only shows you what it wants you to see. We can embrace it or choose to see the truth."

Millie put the last sheet into her basket, picked it up and walked away. Bernice's thoughts drifted from herself back to Ory again, seeing his face riding alone on a dark road. She shook it off and yelled to Millie, "What would you do to help Ory?"

Without turning back, "Me? I'd pray. But you're not me."

That wasn't exactly what she was looking for. She took a breath, formed her lady-like composure, buried what heavy feelings she had exposed, and walked toward the house.

Titaunt sat on the stairs to her home, a cold breeze blew on her face, helping to push her worries to the back of her mind, while also forcing the empty rocker to keep swaying on the porch behind her. She tried to put his face out of her mind, but that scar kept it anchored in view. She hadn't thought about him since her sister died. It was like he had disappeared. She remembered conversations she had with her about Lezin, but her sister never said much.

In the distance Titaunt could see Bernice approaching. As she got closer, all Titaunt could think of was the life they had planned for Ory and how it was all a mistake. Once she arrived Bernice could sense something was wrong, something beyond Ory. She put aside her own intentions for a moment and asked, "Everything okay?"

Titaunt had every right to say no. Most would think she'd be crazy if she didn't. But when Bernice asked her, Titaunt thought of her sister, and what she would say every time Titaunt asked the same question, during the days Lezin was around, and she'd reply, "Everything's just fine." Titaunt always wondered if the two had become involved. If they were hiding things from Ory's father, things that could not be forgiven, sins passed on through the blood of those born from them. And she couldn't help but to think, *What if that's why he killed her?* A conclusion that made the most sense to her. A dangerous situation her sister had been in. Now Titaunt found herself in a deadly place, as well. A man who lost a woman he loved, out for vengeance against the son of the one who killed her, willing to do whatever it took, even if it meant being pushed to insanity. *That's crazy*, she thought. *Impossible.* It was only speculation. But still, there was Sidonie, and she would keep her safe, not provoke the dragon, and let the water calm. So she replied, "Everything's just fine."

Titaunt stood and the two embraced, exchanging kisses on the cheek, then they stood for a moment,

143

settling in to the discomfort. They had never been alone, just the two of them together. Eventually, they talked about the only thing that they ever did. Ory. Bernice said, "They think it was his idea. That he planned it."

"I know."

"He's not coming back, is he? I keep praying that he's going to make it. That he's going to come back to me."

"I think you're praying for the wrong thing."

"Don't you want him to make it?"

"I sure do. I pray that he makes it out alive, that he escapes, and that I never see him again."

"But he'll be safe on the plantation. Once they find he's innocent."

"He'll never be safe on the River Road."

Both so desperately wanted to speak to someone. And now here they were, stuck with someone they had nothing to say to. Well, nothing they were supposed to say. And Bernice never would have, but in the silence she had to think on Ory, and that grew more terrifying by the minute, which is why she was willing to embrace something she was raised not to speak of. The truth. And Titaunt whole-heartedly joined.

"It's funny, people think we are so close because of the arrangement, and perhaps because of things we say of one another, but I've hardly ever spoken to you."

Hugs and kisses exchanged by people who meet are often disingenuous, and those who wear this attractive mask live in a hollow world, starved of connection. Such was the case with many on the River Road, and such was the case with them.

"It's no secret you never wanted us to be married."

"I wanted Ory to have a normal life."

"You don't think I could have given that to him?"

"You don't know what that is. You've never made one decision that was your own."

"I've made choices."

"Of course, about what dress to wear, whether to nap or sing, but about nothing that was your own."

"What about you, sitting alone, taking care of a daughter that is not yours, waiting for a son who doesn't belong to you. I may not have made choices of value, but at least I've done something."

"They would have been alone if not for me."

"A cross you proudly bear."

They were both right. Neither of them had ever heard those words before, and they became so angry because they knew they were true.

"You say I've never made a decision. Well, I decided to love him."

Titaunt laughed, then cried, shaking her head as if she couldn't decide which was the best thing to do.

Bernice spoke firmly, "You mock me?"

"No, sweet thing, I pity you."

"It was a choice…I made."

"Love can't be chosen. It can't be promised. The world doesn't look like it does inside those plantation walls.

145

There's pain. Sacrifice. You're stuck on the idea of Ory, not Ory himself. And when they catch him, when he's gone, you'll fall back behind those walls, sheltered from any true feeling, until someone else comes along to take his place."

With that they both became broken, exhausted from pulling this hard truth out of each other. Titaunt fell to her knees, losing the strength that held her up, that held up her mask. Bernice stood above her. Gutted. Titaunt, with what breath she could control, "It's killing me. This place. And when you understand, it'll kill you, too."

She looked up to Bernice and it was happening. She saw it. And Titaunt was right. It was going to kill her, and it would eat away at her faster than the others, because Bernice's lies weren't hidden, they were believed.

"I'm sorry, Bernice. I would never wish to be you."

Bernice swayed a bit, then walked backwards, away from Titaunt. And like a ghost moving about the world, she floated away.

Bernice was soon walking back on the River Road. Her life lived until then was spinning around in her head. She questioned what things in her life were full and had meaning, and found none. She heard the river call her from over the barrier beside her. She climbed its levee, trekking up its slope to confront it, and when she made it to the top, dark clouds were in the distance, and a heavy wind blew hard, pushing her to a stop and sending waves crashing to her feet. Crawling up the side, the river was high, clawing at the barrier, trying to breach the levee. She felt her breath stolen from her, pulled out by the river, and with each inhale she consciously tried to pull it back in. There she stood, a knowing prisoner to the river.

CJ, who was riding along the River Road, saw Bernice on the levee, fraught with sacrificial thoughts, and he galloped up the levee to her side.

"Bernice?"

He jumped off of his horse, slowly approaching her, arms out as if he would have to reach and grab her at any moment. Bernice yelled against the wind, "Do you think he did it?"

"Bernice, just take a few steps back."

"DO YOU THINK HE DID IT?"

"I want nothing more than for him to be innocent. But they're right, we can't excuse what happened."

"If it is true. If Ory is guilty."

"I don't think Ory's a murderer."

"But if he is."

"Then he goes the way of his father."

His father, she thought. A calmness came to her, her breath steadied, and she stood mustering her strength. The wind spun around her, deepening its gust to a growl, threatening her, warning her, and standing up to it she said, "We're leaving."

"What?"

"We're going after him."

"Wait, we can't just—"

"You go with me or I go alone. I'm telling you because you were once his friend. If he came back your friend, you'll go. They've got no one out there. I don't know if what Ory is doing is right, but I don't know if it's wrong. I only know one thing. He's either like his father because of fate, or because we made him to be."

CJ saw the change in Bernice, he did think she was right, and he couldn't let her go alone.

"Okay."

"No one can know."

Mounting his horse, "I'll meet you soon."

CJ rode off leaving Bernice and the river alone again. The meeting between the two grew in intensity. The river rose, the waves crashed harder, hitting the levee walls as if it were trying to break it down, reaching its white arm out to grab Bernice. And as her face was covered by its misty breath, she commanded, "Let...me...go."

Bernice grew taller, and grew more frightened, but as one final wave slammed into the wall, a crack was made in a levee inside Bernice, and that storm trapped within her caught sight of it, and it began to spin, for it, and not the river, would be the one to breach its barrier.

WANTED MEN

Ory and Will were on their way out of town, nourished and looking to disappear again. Their plan had served them well. The part of two fugitives on the run, one being a slave wanted for murder, didn't become them. They sold themselves well to the town as a man and his property. Will said proudly, "You see, told you it'd work."

Ory smiled and Will smiled back. "You did."

It must have been their way of apologizing. They were comforted again by each other. And the more they realized that they were in this together as partners, as equals, the stronger they would become.

They were just about at the end of town when two men walking their horses were heading in. Ory and Will sharpened their walk, Will hunching behind, Ory guiding. They were getting closer, and once they were within distance of being heard, Ory said, "Good afternoon."

"You, too, sir," one of the men replied.

And then they passed them, continuing into town. Just like that, Ory and Will were in the clear, back into the wild, with less worries than they already had. Ory sighed, and just as he thought, *That was easy*, he heard a voice from behind him.

"Ory?"

He never would have turned, but Ory's guard was down, thinking they had made it. His unfortunate reaction to turn around at the calling of his name confirmed his identity to the men behind him, both with guns drawn. Bounty hunters.

"And that makes you Will," the other man said.

Ory could see the signs now, their swamp stained boots, the long rifle on the horse, their packs filled for a long day's ride. One hunter held the wanted poster of them, comparing their faces with the poor sketch he had before him.

"You know people are looking for you, right?"

The two hunters laughed, proud of their catch. The one with the poster put up his gun and pulled out a rope in preparation to bind them. "Hands up."

They raised their hands slowly. Will could feel the rope already. The hunter might as well have put it around his neck. Ory's mind was racing, he could go for his gun, but one was being held on him. There was nothing he could've done, save for a thing he already did, and he was thankful when he heard a voice yell.

"Over there."

Coming down the road was the Hatter, his clean, pale hat shining in the sun, being guided by the drunkard holding a bloody rag to his nose. Two other law men followed closely behind.

"You see him? The tall one next to that nigger."

The hunter, still with his gun out, slowly moved behind Ory. The Hatter yelled, "Hold it, hold it. Hold it right there."

The Hatter and his company stopped a few yards away from them. His crisp hat was almost blown off by the wind. "God damn it." He snatched it and straightened it back on his head. He pulled his coat back on one side, revealing his gun while fingering his collar, his stance, the stance he always got into when he thought it was time to enforce the law. Most of them noticed that his gun was still buckled into its holster, unable to be drawn even if he wanted to.

"That him?"

The drunkard nodded.

The Hatter asked Ory, "You smash his nose in?"

Ory was unsure how to answer, he didn't want to say anything the hunters didn't like. After all, he did have a gun digging in his back.

"Yes, sir."

"Now why would you do that?"

151

"He was drunk and extremely rude." Ory added, "And he tried to hit me in the face."

Turning to the drunkard as his eyes rolled back, the Hatter said, "Damn it, Bob, you said you didn't do anything this time."

"Well—"

"Oh, shut up." Turning back to Ory, "I'm sorry, gentlemen. This one's always causing problems."

"It's no problem."

"Good day."

Everyone exchanged nods or a gesture of goodbye, but as the Hatter turned away, he noticed hanging from one of the hunter's pockets, the wanted poster. As dumb as this pale Hatter might have been, he knew enough to be suspicious, enough to wonder, *Could it be?* He turned back to them and said, "You know what? On second thought, I think it might be best if we file this as a complaint."

"I don't think that's necessary," said one of the hunters.

"It won't take long. Let's just walk down to the station."

"But I don't think he's broken any laws."

The Hatter tried pulling out his gun, saw it was fastened, struggled for a second, then finally drew, along with the law men behind him. "Neither do I, but this here is my town. So, that means whatever's in it belongs to me.

Now, these two can come with me and you all can be on your way."

"And if we say no?"

"No? Well, then we'll have to take them from you."

"We can split it. Fifty-fifty."

"I like your offer, but, no."

As silence started to descend, all you could hear while these men faced each other was the whimpering sounds of the drunkard slowly backing away. Then, knowing they were at odds, the hunter behind Ory pushed him aside revealing his drawn gun and fired. A bullet hit one of the lawmen in the shoulder, sending blood splattering on the Hatter's face and clean hat.

"Son of a bitch."

It sounded like a canon as their weapons went off almost simultaneously. The hunters ducked and ran in the street trying to dodge the bullets. Ory, who was stumbling back to his feet, grabbed the reins of the horses and headed to Will who at this point was on the ground covering his head. A lawman knelt to the ground and shot one of the hunters in the leg. He fell to the ground, but popped back up, limping as he tried to retreat to his horse. When the hunter got to Ory and Will, Ory noticed behind him the lawman was taking aim, and Ory knocked the gun out the hunter's hand, pulled the hunter's body in close, using him as a shield as the lawman fired three shots into his back. The other hunter, in a fury from seeing his friend killed, ran towards the lawmen in one final charge. The Hatter retreated down the street, holding his gun behind him, firing without looking. As the hunter got close enough to shoot, it was too late. The lawman on the ground who was shot in the arm went unnoticed and when the hunter passed him, a bullet hit him in the back of the head. Ory saw that their fight had come to an end and they only had a little time left.

"Get on, Will."

Ory helped Will onto the horse and slapped it sending him off. He mounted the other and caught up with Will to steady his steed, as they galloped side by side out of the town, chased by angry bullets.

The Hatter whined, "Damn it."

He stopped firing at them riding off. He dropped his gun to his side and huffed. He stood over the two bodies and his wounded officer. He took off his hat, in honor of the dead, but then saw blood on it. His jaw dropped turning to the standing lawmen, "Look at this. Jesus hell."

He threw his hat onto the ground and kicked it down the road, in the best way a plump man could, stomping on it a few times. When he was done, he stopped to catch his breath, looking down the empty road, cursing those bastards that had gotten away.

MAYBE IN ANOTHER WORLD, ANOTHER TIME

Ory and Will managed to escape bullets once again. They were away from the town now, walking their horses off the road, alongside a sugar cane field.

"They're not coming?"

"Two dead, one wounded. We're safe, at least from them."

They came across a well-beaten road, heading east, back toward the river.

"Where does this go?"

"The city's not far down."

Ory knew that's where he would have to go, but he didn't like the thought of heading back to the river. It was time to ditch the horses, but just before they sent them on their way, as Will was raising his hand to slap the horse's butt, Ory thought of something. "Wait. We need to do something first."

In a remote and quiet part of the sugar cane field, Ory and Will stood by each other, and about 20 yards ahead, the horses stood, facing away. Will looked at them, calculating, while Ory grew impatient.

"If you're ever in a desperate situation, which you will most likely be, this is key."

Will tilted his head and squinted his eyes, trying to compute the outcome of this dangerous feat.

"You've got to learn."

"I ride just fine."

Will kept calculating. He was a physical guy, athletic, but that wasn't his problem. His problem was the horse. Would it move? Would it kick? Did he even like being jumped on?

Ory couldn't take it any longer. "Okay. Just watch me. You want to get a nice running start, then just as you get to the back of the horse, jump."

"Master Ory—"

"And as you jump, put your hands onto the back of the horse, lift and guide yourself to the saddle. That easy."

"What if the horse moves?"

"What?"

"He has legs, doesn't he? What if he moves?"

"He won't."

Will didn't look satisfied. Ory rolled his eyes and took off down the road, kicking up dust until he got right up to the horse and did just as he instructed, flying through the air and into the saddle. Ory steered the horse around to face Will and yelled, "You see. It didn't move."

That didn't build his confidence much, but it did challenge him, and he was beginning to feel patronized.

"Listen. If you're scared, you don't have to do it."

Ory hit the right button that time. They both caught a glimpse of those forgotten days when they were younger. A glimmer of words told to them as children, pushing them in the direction of becoming a man. And that's all it would take. Will took off, charging at the horse. His pace quickened, his breath got hard, springing down the road like a wild cat from the brush to his prey. And that was probably his mistake, it's probably what startled the horse. Right when he got to the back, he leapt into the air, soaring through the wind, and sure enough, that horse was spooked and it moved, and Will's body slammed right onto the ground. Ory cringed as Will rolled over onto his back, spitting up dirt.

"Well, maybe we should start slower."

THE PRICE OF A DIRECTION

The Hatter was back sitting behind his desk at the station, feeling defeated, his precious pale hat was now covered in dirt and smeared with blood in his attempt to clean it by rubbing it with his sleeve. Next to him was one of his officers who had his arm bandaged up. The drunkard was on the other side of his desk, dried blood in his nose. They were all looking at the bodies of the bounty hunters that were lying in the cell attached to the room.

The drunkard got an idea. "What if they were drunk?"

"Bob," the Hatter said shaking his head, "Just let us come up with the story."

"Bandits," the wounded one suggested. "Maybe we stumbled on a plot they had."

"Maybe. Sounds complicated. Plot to what?"

They paused their conversation at the sound of someone walking across the porch of the station, the boots were a slow drum thumping, then it stopped at the base of the door. They waited there for a moment, but no one entered.

"You all hear that?"

The knob slowly turned, and as the clouds passed in front of the sun, the door opened and in walked the man of ash, his black hat shielding all but his scar. He closed the door behind him. The cautious Hatter said, "Can I help you?"

"I heard you boys had some trouble out here."

"Ahh...yes. Yes, we did."

"What happened?"

"Well, these gentlemen here, they..." Hoping for someone to jump in, "They were drunk."

The drunkard rolled his eyes and sipped back on his bottle.

"I'm looking for someone. I was wondering if you had come across him."

Once he said that, the Hatter realized, like he did in the road with the bounty hunters, Lezin was after Ory and Will. But, unfortunately for him, the dark man before him was not after the reward that he and the bounty hunters sought. What he was after had no price. The Hatter sat back in his chair and put his feet on his desk.

"I may have seen someone."

Lezin's head shifted slightly, as if he had caught a scent, and he walked to the desk and stood across from him.

The Hatter continued, "You see, I think you and I are after the same thing. Maybe we can work together."

"I don't want any trouble."

"Woah, woah. No, no one wants any trouble."

From behind Lezin came the other lawman from another room, his gun drawn.

"Especially someone in your position." The Hatter enjoyed his second chance. "Now, what I am talking about is a business proposition. What if I said, the information I know comes at a small fee?"

"You file a report, yet?"

"On what?"

"On what happened to those men?"

"No. I'm still working on that."

Lezin pulled his jacket aside revealing his gun. The drunkard, the wounded officer, and the Hatter all sat up, the lawman from behind raised his gun, pressing it to Lezin's back.

The Hatter cautioned, "Hey, no one has to die here. Calm down."

"Oh, no. Someone's got to die."

"What, WHAT? No, no…no, no one does. You can just leave."

"Can't happen. It's already started."

"Are you crazy? Get out of here, mister."

Lezin spun around grabbing the gun pressed to his back while at the same time pulling out his own gun, putting it under the lawman's chin, and firing. Blood hit the ceiling. The drunkard got up and went for the door, but just before his hand reached the knob, Lezin put a bullet through his palm. The drunkard fell to his knees screaming, but not for long, because his cries went silent as another bullet hit him in the throat. The bandaged officer sat in his chair, frozen in shock, but the Hatter was already on his feet, heading out the back as fast as he could. From under Lezin's coat, he pulled out his long, rope-like whip, its end fell, uncoiling to the ground, and he flung it over his head and around, then snapped it at the Hatter, coiling it around his neck, yanking him back and slamming him to the floor. Lezin pulled the Hatter toward him, his belly spread wide as he slid on his back until he was right under Lezin. He straddled the Hatter's chest and tilted his black hat up so that he could see his face.

"I am sorry about that."

"What the hell are you doing?"

"Where did he go?"

The officer in the chair began to move, slowly reaching for his gun, thinking he could get to it while Lezin dealt with his boss. But as he reached for it, Lezin saw that the Hatter noticed his officer going for his gun, and without even taking his eyes off of him, Lezin held up his gun and put a bullet through the officer's skull.

"Where did he go?"

"I'm not telling you anything."

Lezin put the barrel of his gun to the Hatter's belly and pulled the whip around his neck tight.

"Listen, you're already in the grave. You only have one choice left in your fat little life. How quick do you want to get there?"

He pulled the hammer back on his gun and once those serpent eyes peered deep into him, Lezin knew, the Hatter would tell him everything, and his life, the life of his men, and the stupid drunkard, were taken. That was the price they paid for withholding the only thing they knew. The direction Ory rode. Something Lezin could have deduced without him, and he knew it.

On the cue of one last gunshot, Lezin walked out of the station looking out to the empty street, and in no rush at all, slowly walked off the porch and down the street, out to the edge of town. Once he got there he met up with his two silent minions, waiting as always for his command. But they weren't the only ones. Lezin had employed the help of the Bertran boys, who didn't need much coaxing, and they were there, too.

Jean was eager, "So, did you find anything?"

"Enough."

You see, Lezin didn't need the Bertran boys, in fact, he was probably worse off with them. But they provided him with a great alibi. Cogan didn't want Ory and Will back alive, and what better way to provoke them than with three men who would beg for their blood on their hands? Besides, if anything became tricky with the law, they would be there to take the fall.

"I do know Ory has killed two, maybe," counting on his fingers, "six men in town." One of Lezin's dark followers approached him on his horse and Lezin ordered, "At least, make sure that is what the town comes to believe."

Lezin handed him a badge that had *U.S. Marshal* on it and he road off, back into town. Lezin got on his horse like the rest of them.

"We're going to head east, toward the city. They aren't far."

The Bertrans got charged each time they heard they were getting closer, unaware of this spell of revenge that they were under. Lezin would keep them under it, fueling their desire, keeping them blind to his possible plan, one that could go deeper than even he would know.

CURSED MEN

"I have never seen a horse do that, I swear," Ory said, laughing as they stumbled into the brush not far off the road that lead to the city. Will wasn't laughing at first, but he joined once he started recalling it, imagining what he must have looked like. They each fell to the ground, exhausted, managing to find a little sense of enjoyment from their small adventure with the horse. "You'll be riding in no time."

"We should do it again."

Ory and Will looked at each other, forgetting about what was after them, telling themselves they had a future, that there was a world far beyond the river, and that they could make it.

"Yeah, we should."

Then, as the reality set back in, Ory stood, reminded of what he had to do, and the impossible odds that were against them. He was going into the city, on a search for someone who possibly didn't even exist. But they needed help. Their journey was not planned.

"So, what am I supposed to do?"

"Just stay here. I'll be back to get you if I find anyone."

"Like who?"

"People who have experience with these sort of things."

"How are you going to find them?"

"I don't know."

Will stood silent for a moment, holding back on an impulse that he had and thought, *Should I tell him?* There were things told by slaves that were never spoken to white people, or even repeated if not in a safe place. The slaves protected them with great secrecy. But for Will, there were no more slaves, and Ory wasn't most white people.

"Maybe I can help."

"It's too dangerous if we go together, you—"

"No, that's not what I mean. I've heard a few things among the other slaves. They were always talking about different plans, and ideas, and ways to get out. I remember a phrase. Friend of a friend. They say it's a code, a safe word used with the kind of people we're looking for."

"Okay."

"Oh, and…a candle in the window of a house. If you see one. It might be connected to…whatever we're looking for."

"Good. Thank you."

It was a combination of things that took Ory by surprise. The bond Will had with his people, and the giving up of that information. Yes, Will had reason to feel safe in telling him, but it meant something. That trust between the two continued to grow. And the empathy would grow as well, with each story they told, with each honest moment that one had with the other. Ory looked down to the weapons about him. "I sure can't carry these in the city."

Ory unstrapped the harness from around his back and, like a coat, took off the holsters. He put them on the ground near a few bags that they had taken off the horses. But before he let go of the Colts, Ory saw Will's eyes catch them.

"I don't guess you have used one of these before."

"No."

"Yeah, didn't think so." Ory shook his head at his stupid question. "Right. Here, hold it."

Ory took one of the guns and held it out to Will. He grabbed it. It was the first time he had held one and he could feel its weight and power.

"Now, I don't expect you'll use this. You'll be safe until I'm back."

Will just stared at the weapon. Ory might as well have given him a rock for bashing someone's head in, because Will would have looked at it just the same. He held something that could take a man's life. Ory stood on side of him, grabbed Will's hand and held it out. "Think of your arm as a part of the gun. Pull the trigger from inside you, not in your hand. Guide the bullet from here," Ory put his hand to Will's chest. "Breathe. And squeeze." Ory grabbed his shoulder and made sure Will's arm was straight and strong. "You've got six shots. Make the best of them."

Will was frightened by what he held, but wanted to take control of its power. And as Will shifted back and forth between fear and passion, Ory looked upon him and he could see that daze he found himself in many times. Ory walked in front of Will, in front of the gun.

"Listen, Will. The people after us are coming for revenge, not justice. If they find us, this is what it comes down to. Six bullets. Six chances to stay alive. I am not going to stand here and tell you it's easy. It must be terrifying to deliberately put a bullet in a man. But that is not the case for us. Terror can't stop men already dead." Ory grabbed the barrel and put it to his heart, "Not for us. You understand?"

That's how they would have to think of themselves, if they wanted to stay alive. Dead men, with the ability to makes choices without holding on to the things that made a person human.

Will lowered the gun, but not his eyes. Those stayed on Ory as Will confessed, "I feel like I killed him. Like I knew what I was doing. Not in my mind, but my spirit knew those hooks were there, knew all it would take was one push, and he'd bleed until he was empty."

"I imagine it would be hard to remember what happened in a moment like that. You shouldn't worry about it. Just block it out."

Ory was not hesitant to supply Will with a remedy he had so often used. And he would try to do the same now, but he wouldn't be able to, because Ory couldn't take one step before Will spoke again. "Do you think we are cursed men, Master Ory? Those around us die."

Then, in a spell, Ory easily slipped away with Will, talking of the demons and ghosts that haunt their minds.

"Somewhere in a dark part of me, I feel, I've already done it. Taken a life. And if it happens, for the first time, I feel I would be numb to it."

Will couldn't shake the thought of them being cursed men. A thought that began to take root inside him. Will then agreed, "You're right. Terror has no place with those already terrified. You can't wet what is already wet. If I ever took a life again, that day will pass through me just as another day hauling cane."

They stood in the silent echoes of their confessions. The fear they shared and the inevitability.

Will gave the gun back to Ory who holstered it, setting it down near their bags. Ory walked to the road, but stopped just before he stepped out to it. Turning back to Will, "I'm coming back. But if I'm not here tomorrow, you keep running. You don't come for me. They can't be stopped. Their numbers will only grow. We can only hope to escape them. But if one of us is caught, it's over. We must remember our hope for each other is to stay alive. If I come for you, or you come for me, while in the hands of the River Road...we have failed one another. We will have thrown away what we have sacrificed ourselves for. So run. But, I'm coming back."

They didn't speak again. It would be another night with a lot for them to think of on their own. Ory left Will in the woods, just off the road. Will stayed there, waiting for Ory to return, and hopefully it would be with good news. Ory walked down the road, toward the city, looking for someone to aid in their journey. And once Ory was far enough away to where he could no longer see the spot off the road that lead back to Will, he hesitated for a moment. He was worried about him.

FRIEND OF A FRIEND

The city was always alive at night, which was good for Ory, walking and searching. He wasn't alone and he blended into the crowds. Men and women dined on the sidewalks, watching the stream of people dance, stroll, and run along the cobblestone streets. Music and the sounds of singing rang throughout the night.

Ory strayed from the crowds every moment he got to examine the houses from a distance, looking at the windows, looking for a candle, but he never found one. Each time he went in and out of the crowd, his doubt grew. It was a silly thing to go on, and he was beginning to realize what he was attempting might be ridiculous. He had no one.

He reluctantly continued his search, but when he left the crowd this time, he noticed a poster pasted to a lamp post. Ory saw it was another wanted poster. He looked back over his shoulder, ripped it down, and continued away from the people. Then he stopped, taken by a woman before him. Sitting on a stool next to an iron gate was an older black woman with long black hair, dreadlocked and knotted, with a purple dress. In front of her was a wooden table with various dolls and cards and trinkets. She drank from a cup that was steaming under her chin.

"Don't like what you see?"

Ory nervously turned away, trying to flee from this witness, and chose to walk down the closest alley he could see.

"Won't find what you're looking for down that way."

Ory stopped. So far he had been completely unsuccessful in his search. He had to talk to someone, even if it meant this woman who was suspicious of him.

"And how is it you know what I'm looking for? Magic?"

"Don't need magic to read you, boy." She sipped from her drink, studying Ory as he walked to her.

"You live in this city?"

"I do now."

"Listen, I need help."

"Don't we all."

She glanced at her money bucket. Ory was already regretting his decision, but he pulled out a few coins and dropped them in. The lady put her potion down, dusted off her hands, and placed them on the table in front of Ory. "Okay, give me your hands."

"Listen, spare me the act."

"Act?"

"I need to find someone."

The lady picked her steaming cup back up and leaned against the iron gate. "Go on."

"It would be someone that not many people know of."

"A lot of people are like that."

"I am looking to find someone to help me travel inconspicuously."

"Inconspicuously?"

"It means without attracting attention."

"I know what it means." Studying Ory a little more, "Sorry. Don't know anyone like that."

"No one?"

"I think you're on your own."

Ory was about to admit defeat, but he thought back to what Will had told him. There was no risk in trying it. She either knew or she didn't.

"I'm a friend of a friend."

The lady stopped mid-sip and looked at Ory. He then knew she had heard those words before. She smiled at Ory, thankful that he had said it, and she revealed, "Three blocks up this road, then take a right. Second house on your left. Ask for Harvey Sherman."

"Thank you."

Finally finding what he had been looking for, Ory popped up and walked past the woman, but the lady suddenly set her cup down on the table and grabbed Ory's hand and wrist, pulling it to her face.

"Miss, please."

The woman's mouth hung open as she continued to hold, gazing off into the night. She saw something. Some of his past. Some of his future. And she remained silent, her eyes filled with water, but tears would never come. She knew he didn't need her pity. Then she let go.

"What is your name, boy?"

He hesitated for a moment, then said, "Ory."

He handed her the wanted poster, almost as a sign of faith and trust, the same that she had given to him.

"I will remember it, Ory."

Ory would never know what she saw and he would never see her again. He left her, following the directions that she had given, and the lady watched him walk away. She grabbed her cup and leaned back to the iron gate.

Ory made it to the home that she had led him to, and sure enough, when he arrived, a candle sat in the window. A sign hung at the front gate reading *Sherman.* Ory took a breath and walked up to the door and knocked. The door opened and there stood a scrawny man with a mustache.

"May I help you?"

"Yes, I am looking for Harvey Sherman. Is he here?"

"No, he's not."

The man was put off by Ory's bluntness, but was curious. "May I ask who is looking for him?"

173

This time Ory would not be hesitant in using the phrase. "A friend of a friend."

The man was alarmed, and took a step back. Ory thought that it might not have worked this time or maybe even backfired, because he looked ready to run. But Ory had misinterpreted him, he was just shocked because the man, too, had found what he was looking for.

"Well, friend of a friend, come in."

"Sherman?"

"Just call me, the Conductor."

AN UNEXPECTED MEETING

Under the cover of night, Ory had gone for Will and brought him back to the Conductor's home. They didn't know what his profession was, but his home was elegant and clean, one who could afford the finer things in life. In this place, few would suspect them, and Ory and Will would take comfort in that. They would be safe there until they took to the road again.

The three of them sat around a table discussing their journey thus far, but the Conductor was not surprised by most of it.

"I've been reading about you two, wondering if I could help. But I thought you would have been further along by now."

"You'd help murderers?"

"When you're someone like me you learn not to believe everything you read. Would I be, right?"

Will looked at Ory, but Ory wouldn't look to him. He didn't want to let Will think he had any doubt in him. But in truth, Ory didn't know, and when he put aside his dreams, there was little to justify his reason to go and help a man he couldn't prove innocent. Ory had to trust him.

The Conductor continued, "Well, are you?"

"What?"

"Murderers?"

"We're just two men trying to escape."

"Then, I'm your man."

The Conductor would have to be trusted as well, even though at this point he wasn't giving them much to go on, but who else did they have? The two were interested in how exactly all this worked.

"So, what exactly do you do?"

"I am with a group of men and women who try to provide safe passage for escaping slaves."

"How?"

"A…a railroad."

This was rarely spoken of, and outside those who ran it, and many states that bordered the North, not many knew of it. Especially not those this far south, and not these two. But something like this seemed almost unbelievable to them. How could something so big go unnoticed? Regardless, they were intrigued, and whatever this railroad was, they were eager to get on it.

Ory continued in amazement, "This is bigger than I thought."

"Railroad? I've never been on a train before."

"Well, you see it's not—"

"So, does it stop here in the city?"

"I'm sure it doesn't stop here, Will. Right?"

"Well, actually, yes, but, there's no train."

Will was finding this hard to follow, and Ory wasn't far behind.

"There's no train?"

"Then what's the railroad for?"

"It's kind of a metaphor."

"Where does it start?"

"What's a metaphor?"

"Well—"

"Is there even a railroad?"

"No."

"I don't understand."

"Listen, the railroad is not a railroad. It's just what we call it. It's a series of stations and checkpoints, houses or areas that we know are safe for you to go to. You check in to these places all the way until you make it North, or to a free territory."

Ory and Will stared at him for a moment, somewhere between figuring and confusion.

"So, why is it called a railroad?"

The front door to the house flew open. A woman entered with a man right behind her, and she said, "I think you are right. They must have gone—"

The two stopped at the sight of seeing Ory and Will. The woman was rougher than most ladies they'd seen. One might not have even considered her a lady. She didn't wear a dress, or gloves, her hair was not done up and styled, and she didn't smell of perfumes. She wore pants held up by suspenders over a white shirt, and her dark hair hung long, tied back out of her way. But still, Ory would know who she was as he sunk into her eyes. It was Bernice.

"Oh, I forgot to mention. Your friends arrived the other day."

CJ was behind her, but went unnoticed as Ory approached Bernice silently, as when they met in the plantation not many days before. Those dreams he dreamed in his days up North, when Ory wondered about what she'd look like when he'd meet her again, probably looked like this.

"What are you doing here?"

"I don't know."

He looked over the woman transformed before him and Ory caught sight again of a life far from the River Road, under the shade of happiness. She was dirty, and tired, but full of life, like the exhausted girl that chased him in their youth, doing all she could to keep up. Only now she was right beside him, and not lagging behind. She was the girl he remembered.

They slept through the night and most of the next day, recharging from those sleepless nights that came before. On the evening of the following day, Ory and Bernice sat alone. It was hard to believe that this was the first time they were sitting alone since his return, and unfortunate was there situation. Somewhere, in another life they would talk about the sun, and the breeze, and the simple things that the fortunate blissfully waste away in.

"It was just by chance that we found him. How did you know?" Ory asked.

"Remember our dance?"

"Yes."

Ory then remembered him, the man thrown out of the plantation the night of their engagement party. Bernice even said then that her father was suspicious of him regarding such dealings, something she knew more of than she let on.

"The things they don't tell you, you can always hear through walls and under doors."

These little mischievous qualities that popped up about Bernice were a pleasant surprise to him. He enjoyed her unpredictability. They smiled in silence, until they came back to the scarier things of their current days.

"We heard about those bounty hunters."

"That was close."

Bernice didn't like Ory's casual response. She looked away from him, down at the table ahead of her, not expecting that that would be how he responded. Then she felt the need to question him.

"Did you have to kill them?"

"Kill who?"

"Those men in the town."

"I haven't killed anyone."

"The news is everywhere. They're saying you gunned down six men there."

"Six? They're all dead? When we escaped it was only two and I didn't kill them."

Ory's first thought was of Will and the idea of them being cursed men and Will being right. If it was going to be hard to prove their innocence, it was going to be nearly impossible now.

"Someone's setting me up."

"Who?"

"I don't know."

Someone didn't want him captured, brought back to the River Road to be tried and hanged. Someone wanted him dead, and was creating just reason for making him so. For the first time since their flight away from his home, he saw as clear as he did that dark night on the River Road, a flash of fire and a scar. Ory rubbed his head as his memories began to shift, trying to see those nights with his parents, and the arguments they had involving

Lezin. Ory asked himself, *If him, why would he want me dead?*

Bernice pulled him out of his thoughts and said, "You can leave. You've done what you could for Will. It's over now. He's got others to help him."

"I can't leave."

"Why? You're not making any sense. If he is innocent, like you believe, why go on? There's nothing left you can do."

"I can't explain it."

"Try. It can't be any crazier than you already sound."

"You'd be surprised."

"Ory, he doesn't need you."

"I know." Ory looked at Bernice, contemplating if he should do it, and then he did. "I need him."

Maybe he felt he owed her, or somehow wanted to honor her with something he had yet to tell anyone, or maybe he just wanted to talk to someone. Maybe he felt safe with her.

"Under any other circumstance, I never would have done this. But I believe, I don't know how, but... somehow, I feel like I can change the past."

"What do you mean?"

"Like I can save my mother."

"Okay. That does sound a little crazier."

"Not bring her back, but... My memory of her is changing. Ever since that night with Henri, she's almost vanished, and the more I'm with Will, it continues to change. Something's trying to tell me…something. I can't leave him until I find out what that is." He looked to Bernice, "I'm sorry."

There was nothing that could have prepared her for what Ory had said, or anything that could have made her understand it better, but she believed him. He'd have to stay with Will, and if he didn't, he'd be pulled back, beaten by the River Road, an enemy they now shared. She would have to accept it.

"You'll never come back."

"We can stay alive, maybe. But never on the River Road."

"Where?"

"Maybe out West."

There it was again, that reoccurring image, a happiness away from here. But Ory didn't ask. Not now. He wasn't going to ask her if she could see herself living a life with a dead man.

"I'm sure your father could find someone suitable for you."

"I'm sure he's already started."

"Or, maybe you'd do well somewhere else."

"No. I belong with my father on the planation. It's what I was made for."

The Conductor came into the room, not wanting to interrupt them, but he had to. "Ory. It's time."

Ory looked to Bernice, holding back so many things that he wanted to say, things during any other time he could never find the words for. He said none of them.

"I'll see you at the next checkpoint."

Ory walked into the front room where everyone was waiting. Will stood fresh and charged, ready to continue their run.

CJ also looked ready to go, to join them. "I'm going with you."

"No, CJ. Do me a favor. Make sure she stays safe."

CJ wanted to help, even though he was terrified by the idea of being caught with them, but he felt it was the right thing to do. He'd watch Bernice, but reluctantly, because there was building in him a feeling that there was a lack of appreciation for his presence. But right now, he wouldn't let it get to him.

The Conductor was ready to open the door. "Do you remember the location?"

"Thirty miles, a town with a red dirt road through it, there's a barn in the far northeast corner."

"I'll wait for your message at the inn."

He opened the door and they stepped into the doorway next to the Conductor.

"I don't know what to say."

"You don't say anything. When you're safe and far away, you can write."

"I look forward to it."

Will chimed in, "Ory will write one for me."

It surprised them all. Will, the one who was in the deadliest of situations, whose life was being threatened the most, told a joke in the doorway to hell, putting them all at ease. After slight laughs and smiles, Will lead the way out the door and Ory followed behind.

Bernice came to the doorway and quietly yelled to Ory, "Take this." She pulled her handkerchief from her pocket, the only remaining thing that resembled her former self. Ory may have enjoyed her in this current state, but she was still a lady. Delicate, with a fragile heart. And at this moment, she was the one who had read too many stories of princesses trapped in towers, waiting for a knight to come riding through the darkness to save her, and before he'd leave to fight the dragon that imprisoned her there, she'd give him a token to remember her by, for luck. She thought herself silly for doing it. Ory took the handkerchief from her. He would cherish it until the end of his days, even if they were few. He took one step onto the porch, and stopped. There was one thing that he could find the words for, and he turned back to her.

"Bernice. You were made for more."

And after one long extended exhale slowly pulled from her as they walked away, they were gone. The three remaining stood in the doorway, as if they could still see them in the empty road ahead.

CJ asked, "How many people have ever made it using the railroad?"

"From the deep South? Not many."

Bernice said with shaky confidence, "They'll make it."

They returned inside the house and closed the door. It wouldn't be long until they, too, would leave, meeting them in a day or two. But they would travel open and freely along the road under the bright star of day, thinking of those struggling to find the shadows. They were heading for a town that most professional hunters wouldn't think they'd be, which meant all those who tried to search for them there would be amateurs and fools.

THE TOWN OF THE RED DIRT ROAD

In the town of the red dirt road, things were still. There was one of everything. One bar, one grocery, one doctor, and the townspeople that resided in it, a lot considering its size, all frequented these places, proudly supporting each other, living as one family. They stuck together and stayed inside the town and out of trouble, out of the business of others, especially newcomers and passersby.

A newly purchased wagon, painted finely along its wooden side, rolled along the red dirt into town, gracing the place with the arrival of the driver and the men that accompanied him. Behind the reigns was a young man with a finely trimmed goatee and a big smile. Trigger was his name, and he considered himself the leader of these men, this bunch. He drove with one man sitting next to him and four others on horseback following behind. They were the Royals. Men from the North. Younger men looking for adventure in the Savage South, as they called it. As they rode in, they all took deep breaths, enjoying each inhale, as if they had never taken in fresh air or open space before. They all smiled. Occasionally, they'd look at each other and laugh, and smile bigger. They were young men, not much younger than Ory and Will, but men who had lived under brighter skies.

The wagon stopped in front of the inn, the only inn. Trigger's nice clean black boots slammed into the red dirt. He looked around taking in the quiet town, feeling its heartbeat from inside its shops, but also noticing a strange disconnect that he felt from it. They rode in expecting wide eyes and interest at their arrival, being that they were men who had traveled from a place far away. Instead, what few people that walked the streets never took notice, never turned their heads, and went about as if nothing was different. Trigger looked around a moment more, trying to discern why they weren't greeted differently, then he turned to his followers, "Remember, boys, they're a simple people."

His men all nodded in agreement. They tied their horses down. One of the Royals cleaned his smooth saddle down with a white cloth, wiping away dust and dirt. Another brushed the back of his horse, keeping the hair nice and straight, and one fixed his hat while looking at his reflection in the window of the inn. When they where done tending to their appearances, they grabbed bags from the wagon and entered the inn.

Like the rest of the town, the inside of the inn was quiet and unaffected by the Royals' entrance. They approached a gentleman who sat behind a counter reading, holding his post as the gatekeeper to those who entered the town, knowing all that came in an out. Trigger placed his hands on the counter in front of the man, "Rooms please."

The man squinted his eyes and looked at the men, suspicious, as he was with everyone who came in. "What brings you all to town?"

"Business."

"Not much business to be had around here. May I ask what kind?"

"You may not. It's of a professional matter. Information to which you are not entitled."

The man looked at them a bit more, sure of only one thing, judging by their clothes and appearance, they could certainly afford the room.

"Name?"

"Trigger."

The man looked at him as if he was joking, but could tell by Trigger's proud face that he was anything but.

"How many?"

"I am sure you can count, sir."

Trigger smiled at the man who lowered his head and turned around to grab the keys. Trigger looked around the room, taking in again the new scents he was being exposed to, admiring the sparseness of the place. Only one picture hanging, a hall built by no master carpenter, straight lines everywhere. *So simple,* he thought. The man behind the counter handed the keys to Trigger, who passed them along to his company.

"Thank you, sir. Oh, and," Trigger took off his black boots and slammed them down on the clean counter before the man, red dirt that was caked on the bottom crumbling off. "See these get cleaned, will you?"

The Royals made their way to their rooms. The man was left alone again, with Trigger's boots dumped on him to clean, and oddly he felt obligated to do so.

Trigger stood in his room fixing his tie and hair in the mirror, his black coat hanging neatly off to the side. The rest of the group sat around relaxing after their long ride to town. One of them, who sat looking out of the window down onto the town, turned to their leader, "So, Trigger, why didn't we tell him why we were here?"

"Timing. Timing is everything in our line of work."

The Royal nodded his head, taking in the information like an eager student.

"Tonight they'll know."

"Same routine?"

"Same routine."

Trigger grabbed one of the bags that was rolled up like a rug and threw it on the bed. As it landed, the bag unrolled and displayed an arsenal that they had carried in. Rifles, revolvers, and knives, all clean and polished, and most importantly, hardly used. His men gazed upon the weaponry, eager to caress the steel and wood again.

These men were vain and rude and cared little for those they didn't consider to be of their class. This had nothing to do with their origin, being from the North, but everything to do with their spoiled upbringing, instilling in them a sense of entitlement.

The Royals dressed themselves up in the weapons, helping each other in making sure they were all on straight, being sure to look professional. However, their idea of what they were supposed to look like, belts perfectly set on the hip, revolvers equal distance apart, rifles held tightly and carefully, was different than what armed men actually looked like. Men who carried weapons everyday, with ease, like true professionals, which the Royals did not.

"This definitely beats studying law."

"Law school? How about the smell of everyone's garbage and sewage in the streets?"

They laughed and cringed, thrilled with their new found career.

Trigger spoke over them, "Gentleman, bounty hunters must never get excited. They must remain calm and collected."

Bounty hunters. Most boys, most men, who have dreams of another life, one fraught with danger and adventure, saving women in distress, never actually leave their lives for those of their dreams. But these men did.

How dead they must have felt to leave safety and security behind. Or how spoiled were they, not to see that what they had was good.

Trigger, now with a set of revolvers on his hips, put on his black coat, straightened it, and made a final adjustment to his hair. He picked up his hat, ran his fingers around the brim, over the lettering stitched on the inside, *Northern Retailers*. He placed his hat on his finely combed hair and gave himself his last evaluation in the mirror. Trigger then pulled from his inside coat pocket, a folded poster and opened it.

"Time to go to work."

It was the wanted poster with Ory and Will's sketches on it. Trigger studied the faces for an unnecessarily long time, then folded it back up and put it back in his coat pocket.

When you're a child, you only think of the adventure, the days won, the wind in your hair, living wild and free, being a hero to many. Then you get older, and all those days become mixed with the truth, the sad truth of loss and pain, that not every day is won, that the wind is not always at your back, the truth that heroes often die. Maybe that's what the Royals never learned. The stories they heard as children never changed as they grew. Men who never knew loss, men who were...bored. They searched for this new life born out of storybooks, one they thought honorable, protected by a shield of righteousness, and full of reward. But the stories they heard never told of the River Road, and they were blind to their path which was leading them right into the fray.

THE DARK RED SHOWN UNDER THE MOON

The moon was full and high, casting a cold pale light over the sugar cane. Ory and Will walked alongside it enjoying the light that guided their way. They would not argue that this was an easier start than their last one. Most of their walk went without words, not because they had nothing to say, they were just humbled in thought by the friend they had made and those that came to their aid.

Will said, "So, no railroad?"

"No, doesn't look like it."

"That would have been something."

They laughed, walking along, feeling safer than they normally did. The light helped. Then a voice echoed from down one of the entrances to the cane. "Come on, let's go."

Ory and Will jumped into the cane field and became stone, listening for the voice again. They listened hard, and slowly, as their ears began to sharpen and focus in, they could hear the sounds of walking and chopping.

"What is that?"

Will knew immediately. Ory should have known, too, but for him, it wasn't as familiar as it was to Will. Will slowly poked his face out of the cane, looking up to the sky, and the light from the full moon hit his face. "Full moon out tonight. We don't stop on a full moon."

Ory looked into the cane, towards the stomping, the hacking, and the yelling. The danger.

"Stay here."

Ory crawled deeper into the cane, creeping closer to the sound. He could see an opening ahead of him. His pace slowed, he lay on his belly, and peeked his head out into the light ahead. All along the cane he saw a long line of slaves, hacking down, binding up, and hauling cane away. Ory could see their foreman, the man who had been yelling, walking up the line toward him. He snuck back into the cane and was still until the man had passed. Ory turned, crawling through the cane back to Will. "We can't cross the road here. We'll have to go further—"

Ory was sure this is where he had left him.

"Will?"

Ory jumped out to where they had been walking before. There was no sign of him. He feared that someone might have found him. If that were the case, he would be taken closer to the other slaves. Hopefully he was just hiding somewhere, but Ory couldn't take that chance. He made his way down the alleys of cane, back toward the slaves.

He turned the corners of a few empty alleys, getting closer with each step to a man who'd love to catch them. As Ory made his next turn he spotted Will, standing in the middle of a small lane, stiff. Ory ran up to him and grabbed his arm.

"Will."

He tried to pull him off the road, but it was no use. He was posted in the ground. Before Will was a wagon. It was overflowing with cane, but kept in tight by three solid wooden planks running across it, held up by big iron wheels. There was more to this wagon. A set of chains were hanging from it, one extending from each side, giving the ability to put a body against it, spread its arms wide, and bind it to the wagon.

"Will?"

Blood dripped from the chains as Will moved forward, and as he got closer to the wagon, the moon's light revealed it newly painted, drying to a black red that existed only under this night's light. Will held his hand out to it, and pressed it against the wood. It wasn't as dry as he had thought. The coat was thick, so much so that when Will removed his hand, it rolled down his palm and passed his wrist.

Ory approached Will. What was he to say? It was a moment that had completely separated them. But they were not safe, and Ory put his hand to Will's shoulder.

"We have to go."

Will acknowledged Ory with his slow steps away from the wagon. He never took his eyes off of it until they had moved away, outside of the cane, making their way far from that place.

Ory couldn't understand, there was no comprehending what Will saw or felt, though he would try. It reminded them both where they had come from and who they were. All the strides they had made in understanding one another disappeared in that moment, and they had never felt more different and more distant.

AMATEURS AND FOOLS

The same full moon hung over the town of the red dirt road, its residents functioning under their normal habit, keeping to themselves. On this evening most of them congregated in the town's saloon, its one saloon. They all sat around speaking quietly and cordially to each other, enjoying their simple pleasures.

From the other side of the saloon's swinging doors were dark shadows of men, looking in at the people, shifting about each other, and then they became still. The shadow in front took a deep breath. Then two of the figures switched positions, whispering, "I'm supposed to be on the left."

"I thought we were changing it?"

"Alright, quiet. You all ready? Okay, remember, I go first, wait one and a half seconds, then you all follow."

The doors to the saloon swung open, most of the place went silent as the townspeople turned to them.

197

There seemed to be a collective sigh that came from all of them, as eyes rolled, heads shook, and their drinks came down on the tables. The Royals walked through, all wearing their sharp black suits and hats, armed with the polished revolvers and rifles that glistened in the light of the bar, strolling with their noses high, as if they owned the place.

Despite being self proclaimed bounty hunters, and complete novices, they were big men, which made the townspeople a little uneasy. One Royal kept spinning his revolver in and out of its holster, like a child with a toy. Most of them weren't even sure if the Royals had ever fired those weapons before. Trigger was the one who had walked out first, exactly one and a half seconds before the others. He smoothed over his finely trimmed goatee with his finger and thumb and smiled big, proud of his position he had over these men, and he felt a sense of invincibility among them. Trigger pulled out the wanted poster and placed it on the bar, the one of Ory and Will and the reward.

"You," he yelled at the bartender, "Have you seen these men?"

He approached Trigger slowly, throwing his white towel over his shoulder, looked down at the sketches, thought for a moment, then shook his head. "No, sir. Ain't no one like that around here."

"Well, you let me know if you see them." Trigger turned around and yelled to the entire saloon. "You people hear that?"

Trigger stepped onto a chair, then on top of one of the tables that people were drinking at. The rest of the Royals, the ones that weren't already holding rifles, pulled out their revolvers. The place was silent. Again, people leaned back in their chairs, propping their heads up with their arms on the table. The sheriff himself, who had been drunk for hours, placed his face on the bar and went to sleep.

"Anyone hear anything about these two criminals, you best let us know. I don't know how you do things in the South and I don't care. I better get your cooperation. These are dangerous men. You wouldn't want to get hurt. And if you see us in the streets, you best move out of our way."

Trigger looked around to the townspeople, who were dumbfounded by their ridiculousness, sitting wide-eyed. He took that as understanding. He took one more second to enjoy standing on his table stage, then as if he had bowed, he said, "Thank you, thank you. You can all go back to your drinks."

He jumped off of the table, fixed his clothes, and straightened his hat. Trigger and the rest of the Royals found a table for all of them to stand around. Two of the Royals brought them all beers, and another said to

Trigger, "That was amazing, Trigger. It was the best I've ever heard it."

"Yes," he agreed. "I know."

"So, what now?"

"We'll stay at the inn here for a day or two. If we don't hear anything, we move on, if we do…it's dead or alive."

The Royals drank there for the rest of the night and slept at the inn. The same inn that the Conductor was heading to, the place that Ory was to meet them. In a perfect world, the competence of the Royals would suggest that Ory and Will could slip right by them, but that would all depend on the manner in which they arrived.

LIES ON THE ROAD

It was early the next morning back in the city. Most people weren't up yet, but there were some sparks of life from those early risers, mostly men and those opening shops. The Conductor and the rest would be leaving soon. But CJ was sent to check with the city's marshal, to see if there were any new developments regarding Ory and Will, to make sure nothing was going to get in the way of their plans. He did so, and there wasn't much that had developed. Ory and Will looked to be safe for now.

CJ walked out of the marshal's office and watched the slow movings of the early morning. A white wagon rolled through, going over the stones at such a slow pace, the wagon, too, was waking up. A few men with walking canes, one of which rested his on his shoulder, casually passed by setting the flow of the street's current. CJ was alone for the first time in a while. He wondered if what he was doing was the right thing. He was helping fugitives.

Something he himself could hang for. And what would he have gained?

Then, as if he had fallen into a bad dream, "The sheriff know you're here?"

Men were all around him. The Bertran boys, the servants of Lezin, and the man of shadow himself. CJ wondered how long they had been standing around him, he had been thinking for some time.

"I thought your daddy thought it was better to stay behind?"

"I guess I don't listen to everything my daddy says."

"Well, that makes two of us."

Lezin lit a smoke and tilted his hat down, shielding his eyes from the rising sun. Jean stepped in right next to CJ with that impatient quality that many hated him for.

"What do you know about Ory?"

"Don't know anything. Same thing the marshal's office knows. You?"

"Think I'd tell you?"

"We all want the same thing."

"Do we?"

"To catch Ory."

"To catch him and…?"

"To bring him back."

"Hmmm. Nah. I think we can do better than that."

"It's the law."

"The further you get from home, that badge don't mean shit. Out here, you're nothing."

Lezin intervened, "Shut up, Jean. Why don't you all give me and Mr. Clement some time to talk."

Jean was aggravated as usual, being told what to do. The men left, but not before Jean got right up to CJ's ear, bit his bottom lip, then whispered, "Do me a favor. Be there for me when we find him."

CJ was starting to feel, deep in his bones, that it was going to be impossible for Ory to make it back alive, but he still held on to his hope. He believed in the law. And that's what Lezin would play on.

"Those boys, they're something else."

Lezin offered CJ a smoke and he took it. Lezin even fired up a match and lit it for him. They stood smoking for a while. Thinking. Watching. Then, slowly, the dragon changed, and he became soft and sympathetic, looking for help from CJ. "I don't know what to do, CJ. I've tracked many men, but nothing like this. I'm going to be honest. The River Road doesn't want him back."

"Well, the River Road doesn't always get what it wants."

"I'm afraid it does. There's more than you know. Ory is not what he seems."

Lezin had CJ's attention. It wouldn't take much for him to sway CJ. He was already looking for an excuse to change course.

"Mr. Lasseigne didn't want many people knowing. The family has enough problems already. But you being a crucial part of this chase, I feel you have to know."

CJ was beginning to feel valued. To feel important. He turned, open and ready to engage with Lezin in this conversation.

"This was planned."

Of all the things Lezin could have said, that is not what he expected. CJ wanted to take a step back, retreat from this open position he was now in. "I don't believe you."

"It's true. He fooled everyone. It was his plan since he got back. It's why he came back. He hates this place."

"But what about the wedding?"

"You were the Best Man in a wedding that would never exist. You were used to make everything seem real."

"How do you know this?"

"Mr. Lasseigne received a letter from up North, warning him to be careful, because Ory had been influenced by some radicals up there. Mr. Lasseigne asked Ory about it the night of the engagement and Ory, of course, denied it at all. But Ory knew that they were on to him, that he would have to move fast. He wasted no time, and he left that night."

"And Henri?"

"Part of the plan. Sad, I know."

Lezin could see on CJ's face that he got him, that he believed every word. No, it didn't take much, and Lezin was not done yet.

"I am sorry, CJ." Lezin put his hand on his shoulder and gave a squeeze. "It's got to be hard to find this out. But you needed to know."

"No. I appreciate you telling me."

"I know I can trust you to keep this between us. Between men."

"Of course."

Before this, CJ thought of the other night when he went completely unnoticed when he met Ory again. How he was so fixated on Bernice. How Ory didn't even want his help, even though he was putting his own life in jeopardy. But all that was packed down deep, and anger brewed inside him. Not to be seen was bad enough, but to be used and treated like a fool, and to care more for a slave…

Lezin threw his smoke into the street, looked around to make sure no one was watching, and he leaned in, "I am not actually even here to check with the marshal. I'm following up on something else."

"Really?"

"Maybe it might help you put some things together."

"Yeah, maybe. What is it?"

"There's a man in town that shares Ory's beliefs. Harvey Sherman. You know him?"

Lezin was sure to watch every second that passed in CJ's eyes until he gave his answer. And as CJ covered shock and surprise, he acted casual and nonchalant. Lezin saw it all, and he knew before he even answered.

BENJAMIN BOUCVALT

"No, I don't."

This was the answer that Lezin had hoped for. CJ was a smart man, but the stress of the current plight had gotten the best of him and put him out of his wits. Or maybe he didn't know that Lezin was in the shadows of the plantation when he helped throw Harvey Sherman out of it. Or maybe he thought Lezin assumed his father, the sheriff, never told him anything, when in fact, he just got the better of CJ.

"It was worth a shot."

Lezin was about to leave, but before he'd go, he would put on his greatest act of all.

"I just don't want more people to die. So many have gone already."

"Do you think that'll happen?"

"I know it will. And I would hate to be the one who knew something but didn't say it, to have to live knowing I could have saved lives if I would have just said something."

CJ took one last inhale of his smoke then threw it into the street. He breathed it out slowly and turned to Lezin. He knew what he had to do, but when he looked into those dark eyes hidden in the shadow of his brim, CJ no longer had a choice, and all the feelings he had before ran from his mind as he was overcome by fear.

THE LIGHT AND THE LION

It was well into the afternoon and the two had been walking most of the day. The event from the other night made Ory cautious about saying anything. Will wasn't saying much either, which left them to their own minds, the thoughts and bitterness they had. In the silence Ory thought of Bernice, and a growing feeling he had for her, thinking how it was all in vain, and a life with her would not be in his future. But Will, his mind was elsewhere, dwelling on darker things.

Ory could see that the road's dirt was starting to turn red. The town was getting close. Soon they would be at their checkpoint and maybe there they could regroup and relax. Clear their minds. Ory mentioned, "I'm looking forward to another safe night."

Will made no reply, adding to the tension of the day, but Ory accepted it. The road had then become a solid red, and as Ory took notice he said to Will, "Okay, the town is just up ahead. Let's get off the road and go through the woods to the barn."

Will, again, made no reply and just kept walking. That was the start of it. Ory gave Will his time, but he couldn't stand for this. Will was being stubborn. They needed to get off the road. His defiance made it dangerous, and made Ory anxious. It was making him angry.

"Will. Get off the road."

Will stopped, but he didn't turn around to look at Ory. "Yes, sir."

Ory would have gotten a sense of relief from that, but it was too late. Two men were coming up the road from behind them, heading into town. Ory and Will had to think fast. They couldn't jump into the woods now, and they wouldn't be crossing these men, they were headed in the same direction.

"Okay, Will, keep walking. Remember, you're my slave, so get behind me."

Will didn't look satisfied with this plan, and being reminded that he was Ory's slave didn't sit well with him either. They walked down the road toward the town, but at a slow pace in hopes that the men behind them would be moving faster and would pass them up before they hit the town, giving them enough time to jump into the woods. It didn't take long for the men to catch up to them. Once they got side by side, one of the men said, "Good afternoon."

"Good afternoon."

Then as casual as the rest, Will joined in. "Good afternoon."

Ory turned to Will in disbelief. The men next to him found this off-putting and offensive, but they didn't say anything and continued walking. The men started to pull ahead, but then Will sped up, getting back in front of them, passing up Ory. They started to think that this was some kind of a joke.

"Your nigger has some liberties."

Unable to think of anything else, "Yes. He does."

Ory needed to cover this the best way that he could. Already Will was making them worth remembering. Ory tried to justify the situation. "He's one of those dumb ones. He's not all there. I use him for small things."

Fury ignited behind Will's eyes.

"Got to put those like him down."

Will interjected, "You should be put down."

"What did he say?"

"Nothing."

"I said," Will stopped and faced the man, "people like you need to be put down."

"Listen, sir, you won't keep your nigger under control, I will."

The man grabbed Will by the shirt and raised his hand, but Will quickly hit him in the throat. He choked and brought both hands to his neck. Will then punched him in the nose and he fell to the ground. The other man, coming right from behind his friend, pulled out a knife and swung it at Will, but Ory jumped in between the two trying to stop the fight. He failed and the man's swinging blade sliced Ory's palm as he held it up in mercy. Ory pulled one of the Colts out with his other hand and put it to the man's head.

"Leave."

The man stepped back, sheathed his knife, and picked up his friend who was now bleeding down his face and they ran to the town. Ory holstered the Colt and they sprung into the woods.

They stumbled into a small open area in the woods, still concealed by the shadows of the trees. They threw their packs down and caught their breath. Ory ripped a piece of cloth from inside one of the bags and wrapped his hand. Will looked at it. There was a lot of blood.

"You okay?"

"Fine."

Ory finished tying up his hand and paced around the area. Will could tell that Ory wanted to say something, he badly wanted to speak, as if it was ready to burst out of his mouth. But instead, Will said, "They'll find us."

"Us?"

"They'll catch us sooner or later."

Ory stopped his pacing. He felt the urge to separate himself from Will. This idea of *us* was getting to him.

"What was that back there?"

"What was what?"

"What are you trying to do?"

"Nothing."

"Do you all of a sudden want to get yourself killed? I'm trying to save your life."

Ory tried to see it the way Will did, what it must have been like for him, but Ory couldn't see that. Like the night before, Ory failed to comprehend.

"I realize what most men do is wrong."

"Do you?"

"Yes. But that is no reason to throw your life away."

"Isn't it?"

"Why are you acting like this?"

"Maybe it's what I should've been doing all along."

"Will, I could have shot that man."

"He deserved to die."

This wasn't Will anymore. Ory didn't see the person he knew from his childhood, he saw someone else, a man capable of much more pain. A man that Ory didn't think he was on the run with.

"You killed him, didn't you? All that bullshit about being cursed, how do I know I didn't show up right after you threw him on those hooks? How do I know you're not just a murderer?"

Ory looked for an answer, for a reason not to believe it, but he couldn't find one. The way Will looked now, he couldn't see an accident. All he saw was vengeance. A man without remorse.

"They would have been after you, but I helped."

His memories were changing again. The old haunting one returned, its cold familiar images, and Ory saw the possibility that this was a mistake, and that the sliver of life he could have had was gone.

"I had a life."

"You're right."

"A life, god damn it. I was getting married, Will, to a woman I love. But I trusted you. Was that a mistake? Please, don't give me a reason to hate you, too."

"You're right. I shouldn't give you a reason. But then, you're just a man with a dead mamma that's gonna end up just like his father."

There was no stopping it now. Ory's head cocked up and back with that serpent-like quality and he shot toward Will, tackling him to the ground. They rolled in the leaves and branches around them, wrestling until Ory found himself on top of Will. He sat up and punched him once, twice, three times. Will's head snapped back from its beating and his eyes focused in as his rage took form and he bucked Ory off him. They wrestled until Will was on Ory, punching him once, twice, three times. Ory grabbed Will's collar and Will did the same, they pulled each other up, wrestling to their feet. Then Will took Ory's body and slammed it into a tree, pressing him hard against it. Ory could feel the jagged bark digging into his back. Ory managed to push off and slam Will into a tree as well, doing the same. Then Will slammed Ory again.

Then Ory, Will. And they went back and forth that way, many times, until their slams became weaker and slower, and they both fell to the ground. Their bodies' limbs lay still as their chests rose high, heaving up and down. They stared through the branches and into the sky. Ory rolled over, crawled and sat, leaning against one of the trees. He looked to his hand. The bandage was now filled with blood.

"I was your friend."

"Is that what you call it? Master Ory?"

Ory looked to Will and had no words.

"No, no, you are. I'm sorry. And now you're upset."

Will brought himself to his feet.

"Is it about your hand? Is it about the pain? I understand. You tried to stop a fight I caused and you got cut. It's about your hand. I see."

Will walked over to one of their packs on the ground, bent over, and pulled a knife out of it. He walked back to Ory, held his hand out to him, then took the knife and dragged it slowly across his palm. Will's face never flinched.

"There, Ory. Now we're even. Now we're both in pain."

Ory watched as Will held it out, blood dripping, not wrapping it, just letting it hang there for Ory to see.

"You know, maybe right now you think I don't care about you, and what you've done. You may be right. But don't you dare sit there, with that scratch on your hand,

and say you did all this for me. Don't pretend like you aren't trying to cover your own damn selfish intentions. Your hand is bleeding, so is mine. Don't we bleed the same? We're no different. I know you're not here for me, because I wouldn't be. Now you're telling me not to give you reason to hate me. Be carful Ory, because I wouldn't want you to give me any reason."

Will threw the knife down by Ory's side. Ory grabbed the knife and saw the blood on the blade, then he looked up to Will. Ory could look at the bloody hand no more. He stood, looked at Will, said nothing, and walked away. Will gazed down to his bleeding hand, and he was sorry. He did believe Ory was his friend. *A friend is honest,* he thought. Will yelled back for Ory, but he didn't hear him. Ory didn't know where he would go or for how long. But he was gone, and they were both alone.

This was the manner in which they arrived in the town of the red dirt road, and what was once the safest town for them to be, was about to become one of the most dangerous places of all.

WHEN THE BLACK WALL BREAKS

In the center of the town, on the red dirt road, the Conductor, Bernice, and CJ stood outside the inn, the one inn, not far from the one saloon. The streets were quiet. A few people crossed here and there. Bernice said to the Conductor, "It's getting late."

"I'm sure they made it to the barn. There's no rush for Ory to meet us."

They continued to wait. Not too far down the road, CJ could see a man enter the saloon, a man that looked like Ory. He checked back with the other two to make sure they didn't notice, and seeing that they didn't, he said, "I'm going to take a look around."

CJ walked down the red road towards the bar. Bernice paced nervously, biting her nails.

"Don't worry. I'm sure Ory's just playing it safe. We should look around as well."

The Conductor took Bernice by the arm and escorted her down the red road in the opposite direction of CJ.

Moments after they separated from the inn, from inside it came the Royals, sharply dressed in their black suits and hats, Trigger leading the way as usual. On the side of him were the two men that Will and Ory encountered entering the town. The one man still had blood on his face.

"Are you sure it was them?"

"It was a white man and a slave and I've never seen them around here before."

"Thank you. We'll take it from here."

"You bet you will. And when you find them, you get the hell out of our town."

The two men left them, and it was just the Royals now, walking down the center of the road, in the direction of the fight their informants had participated in, back to the direction of Will.

"This is it boys."

They held tight to their rifles and pulled out their revolvers, and that smile on Trigger's face managed to grow bigger.

Ory entered the saloon. It was empty, save for one man. Ory went straight to the bar, signaled to the bartender, and said, "Bourbon."

The bartender nodded, throwing his white towel over his shoulder. While he was making the drink he took a few extra glances at Ory. He had seen his face before, the other night in the sketches shown to him by the Royals, but he couldn't remember. He brought the drink to Ory.

"Do I know you?"

"No, I'm sorry."

"Are you sure, because—"

"I said, no."

He took the towel from his shoulder, turned around and walked away. Just like the rest of the people in this town. They didn't want any trouble. Ory grabbed his drink, and as he held it to his mouth he noticed the saloon's only other customer next to him, a man passed out with his face smashed against the bar. What caught his eye was his revolver on his hip and the badge on his coat. The town sheriff. Ory shook his head and took a sip.

"Hell of a time to be drinking."

Ory turned to find CJ behind him, walking up to the bar next to him.

"So, you two made it."

"Yeah."

"We've been waiting for you back at the inn."

"I was making my way there. Just had to make a stop."

"I see."

CJ waved to the bartender and pointed to Ory's drink. They sat in silence as the bartender cleaned a glass, made CJ's drink, brought it over, and sat it down. It melted a little before he drank it. Each stared ahead of himself.

"Ory, you can't keep this up. You're not going to make it. You know that?"

"Suppose I do."

"Why didn't you tell me?"

"Tell you what?"

"I thought we were friends?"

"We are."

"Is that why I was your Best Man?"

"Yes."

"Is that why you didn't want me helping you? You were worried about my safety?"

"Sure."

CJ took a deep breath through his nose, took a big swig from his glass, taking in ice and all, bit down one time hard on the ice, then swallowed.

"Why are you lying to me?"

"What am I lying about?"

CJ was getting ahead of himself, a little too rowdy. He shook his head a little, took a smaller, lighter breath. "I can't let you do this. I need to take you in."

"CJ, you don't know—"

"More people are going to get hurt and I can't let that happen."

"Hey, no one is going to get hurt."

"Just like those six men a few days ago?"

"I said that wasn't me."

"Stop lying to me."

CJ closed his eyes, ashamed he couldn't hold back his outburst. It had to come out, though. He had hoped to ease it out, to break it to him gently.

"I know everything, Ory. Stop the lies."

"What lies?"

"I know all about the plan. The one you had made up North."

"What are you talking about?"

"This whole thing. Freeing a slave. Killing a slave owner. Removing anyone in your way. I know all about it."

Ory could see in CJ's eyes that these were not his words and that there was more coming, something out of CJ's control. He didn't know what, but whatever it was, it had a hold on CJ, and he could see the fear in him.

"You didn't?"

"They can help."

"No, CJ, you don't know what's after us."

"Yes, I do. I know more than you think. They are going to help you. You. Need. Help, Ory."

"Please tell me you didn't do what I think you did."

CJ's anger with Ory started to slip, but it didn't come across that way. His voice began to crack and his body began to shake, and the hysteria grew as he went on. "I'm sorry. You've forced my hand."

"What?"

"You may hate the River Road, but you don't have the right."

"CJ, what did you do?"

"If you would have come to me, if you were really my friend and let me help you, this wouldn't have happened."

"What did you do?"

Ory grabbed CJ's collar and threw him against the wall, pulling out one the Colts and pointing it at his chest. The bartender saw this and casually disappeared into the back, as he would always do in these situations. CJ had already been shaking, but was even more so with the Colt's barrel on him.

"Still haven't used those yet?"

"No."

"Well, you better get ready."

CJ fought to hold on to all the things he planned to say, all the reasons he had for Ory, all the things he had been trying to convince himself of, but they left him, and out came the truth.

"I'm sorry. They're coming, Ory."

"Who's coming?"

"I didn't want to tell him. I wasn't going to, whether you were guilty or not. You were my friend. Even though I felt betrayed, I was going to keep quiet. But he knew. He could see inside me. It was as if he ripped it out of me with his eyes. His burning eyes."

"CJ, who's coming?"

"The Bertran boys and…Lezin."

Ory let him go, grabbed his drink from the bar, and smashed it on the wall next to CJ's face. Ory collected himself. He thought of those eyes that CJ had spoken of, then of the terror that once took hold of him.

"So you know, whatever he told you, he said to find me. But not to catch me and bring me back. He's coming to kill me."

CJ stood, thinking on Ory's fate, one that he had already known without Ory telling him. It had been told to him by Lezin's eyes, but he didn't tell Ory that, and he would live in the shame of it.

Walking back into town, right down the middle of the red dirt road, as if they were leading a parade, came the Royals. Guns out, and high, reveling in their excellence, proud of being the best hunters alive. Trigger praised them, "You see, boys, this is what professionals look like."

From behind, with a rope tied around his wrists, they pulled Will. He was bleeding from the side of his head from when they nabbed him back in the woods. Professionals or not, it was six against one, and Will was taken easily. They pulled him along, yanking him every now and then, like a dog on a leash, keeping him heeled at their backs.

"I'm glad to see a murderer like you caught, unable to do harm again. And the reward is going to be nice."

They laughed and continued along the red dirt road. Men and women in the town looked through their windows out to the road, but most shut their curtains. If some were on the street, they quickly vanished inside.

Trigger took notice of Will's beaten face. "What happened to you? You been misbehaving?" He yanked Will right up next to him, examining the cuts and bruises from his fight with Ory earlier. He didn't look long before Will spat in his face, right in Trigger's eye. His gang laughed at him, but quieted up as Trigger turned to them with a snarl. When he looked back to Will he saw him smiling.

"You think that's funny?"

He slapped Will in the face. It didn't affect him much, so Trigger hit him again. Still nothing. Trigger looked to his men. They stood wide-eyed, waiting to see what he was going to do next. His sense of authority was dwindling. So, he pulled out his gun and pistol whipped him, sending Will crashing to the ground. Trigger put up his gun and knelt down next to him. "Do you think we need to bring you back in one piece? Dead or alive, my friend." He grabbed Will's jaw to see if he was registering what he was saying, and saw that he did. "Don't worry, we're going to catch your friend, too. But you've just made doing it a lot more enjoyable for me. Pick him up." The Royals grabbed Will and brought him to his feet, continuing down the red road.

Ory was still at the bar, calculating, CJ still against the wall. Now, knowing Lezin knew where he was, coming with men that could spot him easily, it was dangerous for him to just step out of the bar.

"How much time do I have?"

"They could be here already."

"Where's the Conductor?"

"He's waiting for you at the inn."

"Is the barn safe?"

"Yes, yes. They don't know about it."

"You tell the Conductor to meet us there."

"Ory the best thing for you—"

Their attention was caught by a group of men walking out in the road. Through the windows they could see Trigger and the rest of the Royals parading past the bar, dragging Will behind them.

"They got him." Turning to CJ, "You see what you've done."

Ory grabbed CJ and threw him across the saloon, sending him into chairs and tables. He scrambled to his feet and went to the window.

"No. That's not them. I don't know who they are."

The Royals had passed the saloon and were now approaching the inn, where, across the street from it was a wooden frame shooting up and across about eight feet high, where the town's *Welcome* sign was hanging.

"Over here. This looks like a good spot."

They dragged Will over to the frame and threw him down on the ground underneath it. One of them threw a chain over the wooden cross beam above Will, grabbed the other end hanging down, and locked it to Will's wrists. He pulled the other end and Will's arms shot straight up into the air. He made sure his arms couldn't come down, then tied off the chain to the side of the frame.

"I promise you, I will personally see that murderers like you and your friend are hanged, unable to hurt anyone anymore."

Trigger had been caught in the web of lies spun by the River Road. He stood tall next to Will, reciting these lines of dialogue he had practiced in the mirror since the days of his youth.

Will said nothing. He was alone again, falling back into his prison. He thought of Ory and if he'd see him again. Hoping that their last moments together weren't the end. Trigger thought of Ory as well, and with a distaste in his mouth asked Will, "You two, I bet, are good friends. Maybe even willing to give your life for the other? Let's see how good, shall we?"

The bravest man in the town was the barber, whose shop they were right in front of. He saw what was going on and rushed out into the street.

"Hey, you all can't be doing that."

A bullet smashed one of his windows as one of the Royals shot at him.

"Back in the shop, old man."

Obviously not brave enough, the barber ran back inside and shut his door. The gunshot startled some and alerted others. The Royal who fired the gun was shocked by the glass exploding and the sound it made. The Conductor and Bernice came running out of the inn to see what was happening, and they saw Will strung up in front of them.

Bernice yelled, "Will."

Ory watched them come out of the inn.

"Oh, no. Bernice." Grabbing CJ, "You get her out of there."

Ory threw him out of the saloon and CJ started running toward the Royals. He pulled out his gun with one hand, and as he got closer to them he fumbled to get a hold of his badge, and just as he passed the closest Royal he said, "Hey, you can't be—" Before he could show them his badge, the Royal sent him flying back as he hit him in the face with the back end of his rifle, knocking him to the ground. CJ's body went still.

"This him?"

Trigger examined the wanted poster, comparing it to CJ's face. "It doesn't look like him."

Bernice tried to run out into the road but the Conductor grabbed her and pulled her back. "Bernice, get inside."

Trigger noticed Bernice as he put the poster back in his coat pocket.

"Ma'am, please stay where you are. This is for your safety. We are professionals in the middle of apprehending some very dangerous individuals."

Trigger nodded to one of his men. He pulled a thin wooden rod from the back of their wagon, still parked in the street from the other day. The Royal walked up to Will, did a test swing with his wooden weapon, looked back to Trigger, who nodded, and the Royal swung. Will's face went tight, but he didn't scream, though he wanted to. He saw Bernice, and she looked at him with eyes that he had never seen in her before, wide and red, glazed over in despair. He knew the danger that was in that road, and if he screamed, he knew she'd run into it. Will didn't care much for her safety. She was trying to help, though, she wasn't there for him. In truth, it might as well have been her that put him here. But Will thought there was no need for harm to come to both of them. And Ory. He thought of him and his love for her. For him, he would try to keep her safe. The Royal swung again. He didn't scream. Bernice pulsed forward.

Will said softly, "No," shaking his head to Bernice, "don't."

The Royal swung, lashing Will on the chest, almost hitting his face. Still, no scream. Trigger looked around the town, searching, but saw no one. He nodded for the Royal to continue. Will, seeing the desperation grow in Bernice, "No."

Trigger was becoming frustrated that his plan to draw Ory out wasn't working. He ordered the Royal, "Harder."

He turned to Trigger, thinking he had been swinging hard enough already, and for this Royal, the glamour and glory of the stories began to fade, and he was no longer happy with the place he found himself in. But he listened to his orders and swung his hardest yet, and a snap could be heard clear across town. Still...no scream. But this time, it wouldn't be enough, as the lash broke skin, and blood appeared, running down Will's chest. It was too late, and Bernice was off.

"Stop it."

The Conductor tried to follow her but one of the men had pointed his gun at him, stopping his sprint. Bernice was out in the road, darting for Will, but was intercepted by one of the Royals.

"Woah...calm down, ma'am."

"You're killing him."

"Ma'am, we're dealing justice here."

"Justice?"

Bernice cocked back and sent her fist flying, surprising everyone with the force behind it, and hit him so hard in the face his feet left the ground and his back replaced them. Two other Royals were right on Bernice, each grabbing one of her arms, her legs were flailing through the air. The man she punched stood up, bleeding from his mouth. "Trigger, she knocked out two of my teeth." The Royal spat out his teeth onto the ground, blood coming with it. He went to grab her face, but she swiftly got a hold of his hand with her mouth and bit down hard, breaking skin and ripping flesh. The Royal screamed. "Ah, damn it! Trigger, she bit me."

Trigger yelled, "Knock her out."

The Royals looked at each other, unable to believe what they just heard.

"But, Trigger, she's a woman."

Another concurred, "Yeah, I thought we weren't suppose to hurt women?"

"Now."

Reluctantly, the Royal took his rifle and knocked Bernice on the side of the head with it, rendering her almost unconscious. Trigger had now lost that cool and calm demeanor that he preached to his men, and he, too, was seeing the reality of this world.

"Tie her down."

They dragged her to the porch of the inn, threw her down, and tied her to one of the columns, sitting her so that she faced the road, seeing Will on display. She noticed not far off, behind a barrel in the road, a man with a top hat, staying out of danger, but close enough to get a good look, enjoying the show. Slowly coming back to, with a whisper, "Help us."

The man in the top hat saw her, but ducked further behind the barrel and would not get involved. Bernice turned back to Will. She looked at his bleeding chest and thought back to that day in Ory's home when she had given him up. What she wouldn't give to go back to that day. To go back and stop all this from happening. She looked up to the sky and cried, "I'm praying, Millie. Oh, dear God I'm praying."

There was no one left. CJ was unconscious. The Conductor had a gun to his head. Bernice was tied up and had done all that she could. Will had no one, save the one who looked on from behind the glass in the saloon up the road.

Ory stood, knowing he was all that was left. His dream, his memory, went white, back to that blurred canvas he saw riding with Will. He yelled and held his head, holding it together as if it were ready to explode. He saw the image of Will, bloodied at the base of the bed.

"What are you trying to tell me?"

He cried out, yelling, holding his heart. His eyes seemed to shake inside his head. Then he felt it. It was coming. But he pushed down hard, all the passions, all the pain, all the memories that tried to break through the black wall inside him. Tiny cracks in it began to form, and light started to spill, but Ory pushed down harder, overpowering the light, and just before the wall went black again, he heard a voice in his head, as clearly as if said before him. *Son*. Ory looked around but saw no one. *Son*, he heard again. He ran to the window and looked out down the road to Will, stretched high by the chains around his wrists. *Son*. Ory closed his eyes and saw his father. *Let it go*. His head shook and he squeezed his eyelids shut a moment more.

"I am not him. I will not…become…him."

When he opened them again, it all went still, as life does inside the eye of a storm, and light appeared again in the cracks and they continued to grow, until all that he kept hidden away came rushing forward.

Trigger looked out to Will, feeling like a failure to his men since he couldn't bring terror to the eyes of this man whom they claimed to be a murderer.

"Looks like we need to put a little more effort into it."

"Trigger?"

"Burn him a few."

The Royal put down the wooden rod and pulled out his revolver, he looked to the other Royals, hoping one of them would say something, but none did.

"How bad are we talking?"

"You know. Just graze him."

The Royal aimed the revolver at Will, pulled the hammer back, and just before he pulled the trigger, an explosion came from behind them.

They turned and looked back down the red dirt road as a chair smashed through the window of the saloon into the street. The Royals looked at each other. Silence.

"What the hell was that?"

They waited. Still, it was silent. Bernice was regaining her wits, and she, too, saw the chair fly into the street, and prayed it wasn't who she thought it was. Trigger said, "Go check it out."

"Why me?"

"Go, damn it."

The Royal began to walk, creeping slowly towards the chair, but he didn't make it far before someone walked out of the saloon and into the road. Trigger's smile looked as if he had seen gold at the end of the red dirt road.

"See that? You see, I knew what I was doing all along."

Bernice yelled, "Ory."

"Alright, boys."

"No, stop, please."

Two of the Royals with rifles stepped up to their wagon in the street. Ory stood a ways down the road, but within the range of the rifles. They rested their rifles on the wagon, taking aim, and Trigger ordered, "Drop him where he stands."

She pleaded, "No."

Two shots rang out. The echo from the blast lingered until there was silence. They waited a moment. Ory stood still in the distance. Unmoved. He breathed smoothly, looking at the rough red sand beneath his feet, then he tilted his head up to the Royals, and as if he was moving downhill, he started to walk toward them.

"Holy shit."

"What the hell are you doing? Shoot him."

They both shot again and both missed. Ory's walk sped up.

"Sights must be off."

"Hurry up, damn it, he's getting closer."

Bernice's head fell back as her vision blurred and just before she fainted, a final word slipped out of her mouth. "Please."

The Royals brought their rifles up again, taking serious aim, focusing hard, squinting tight, their fingers slowly gripping the triggers, but just before they pulled, Ory, with both hands, drew the Colts, dropping to his knees, firing two shots, sending two bullets right under the wagon, one in each of the riflemen's legs.

Trigger fell to the ground crawling and hiding behind the wagon wheels. Ory fired two more shots. One hitting the arm of the Royal holding the Conductor hostage, sending his gun flying away, and the other, went into the arm of the one next to Bernice, disarming him, as well. Trigger yelled, "Ambush. Run."

The last Royal ran and hid behind Will, thinking Ory wouldn't risk shooting at him. Ory fired another bullet hitting Will's chains that hung above him, sending his body falling to the ground, now leaving the Royal exposed. His hands flew in the air in surrender. Ory dropped one of the Colts, and with his free hand, rapidly pulled the hammer back five times, using the remaining bullets to break the chain holding up one side of the *Welcome* sign above the Royal, and it swung down, smashing him in the face. Ory dropped the remaining Colt to the ground.

Trigger's smile was gone, and when he saw Ory had no weapons, he was on his feet sprinting down the road.

As he passed the shops, he saw some of the townspeople peeking through their windows. "Help me, you cowards."

Ory turned and walked to the wagon as Trigger was kicking up dust. Ory picked up one of the rifles and rested it on the wagon. He took aim, but Trigger's image was almost gone from sight, it had become no more than a blur in the distance. Ory took a deep breath and heard, *Hold it in and let it go.* He breathed out. *Now squeeze.* Trigger screamed as his face went smashing into the red dirt of the road. The bullet had pierced him in his ass, and he began to cry.

Ory dropped the rifle, turned, and made his way to Will. The Royals moaned and rolled about the red dirt road, crawling away. The man in the top hat popped up from behind the barrel and ran up to Ory.

"That was incredible. I've never seen anything like that. When I was your age, you bet I—"

Once he got close, the man was sent to the ground by a hard punch from Ory's fist. Will was on his knees, looking down to the chains shackled to his wrists. He looked up to Ory, who approached with the sun at his back, slowly coming to a stop, standing above him.

Will said, "You get lost again?"

"Yeah."

"Why'd you come?"

"Some men bleed for the wrong reasons."

Ory extended his hand to Will and helped him up, and as they stood face to face, their hands remained together, the hands once sliced open. Hands mended.

"Ory. Bernice."

Ory ran over to Bernice and with the aid of the Conductor, got her untied.

"Bernice." He cradled her in his arms, and gently tapped her face. "Bernice, wake up."

Her eyes slowly blinked, they searched for focus, and the first thing she saw when she came to was the boy lit by the light on the horizon.

"Ory? I thought I saw you die."

"Not yet."

He pushed the hair out of her face and could see that she would be okay. CJ regained consciousness in the street, waking up to the blood from the wounded around him, failing to see what Lezin had led him to believe he would find, a street that would be full of bodies. But there were none. This murderer managed to keep them all alive.

Ory turned to the Conductor. "You all go inside. Meet us at the barn when it's safe."

They all scrambled and separated. The three to the inn, and Ory and Will out to the barn. As they made their way out of the town, they saw Trigger and his wounded men gathered in fear, backed up against a wall of one of the buildings. Ory picked up Trigger's hat from the middle of the road and approached them. He noticed the stitching *Northern Retailers* on the inside of the hat. As he got closer, Trigger pulled his revolver out and pointed it at Ory, the gun shaking vigorously in his hand. Ory saw this newly born fear swirling in their eyes, men who knew nothing of what they were doing. A truly pitiful sight. Enough people had died already, and Ory would keep them alive if he could. He locked eyes with each of them, one by one. In front of them was a man who would speak deep and true. They saw in Ory what they all thought they saw in Trigger. A man worth listening to.

"Men are coming. Men far worse than me. And now you've become a part of this. They'll be looking for you. Tend to your men. Stay inside. Talk to no one. And tomorrow…" Ory threw Trigger's hat down to him. "Go home."

They would do exactly as Ory had ordered them to. The Royals would eventually make it home, staying alive, glad to reunite with their days of comfort and safety.

Ory and Will had cleared the streets fast. They needed to hide. For what had yet to come, was far more dangerous than this. The men after them were anything but amateurs and fools. What came for them would not miss. It would not hesitate. It would not run. When the dragon found Ory, it would bring fire and ash with it, burning and choking him with a force from the past.

ROAD'S END

On the northeast corner of the town was the barn. Inside it were two men feeling at the end of their road. They sat facing each other in the center of the place, leaning back against a stack of hay and the wooden door of a stall. A good distance was between them, but they could still see each other's faces. They sat there, running their entire journey thus far in the other's eyes. Will looked down to the Colts strapped to Ory's chest.

"I guess some things are worth remembering." Will felt his wrists, "I have never seen anything like that."

"Yeah. That makes two of us."

Will thought of all those wounded men cast out in the red dirt. All the blood.

"You don't suppose after that we're going to make it much farther?"

"Not likely."

Ory saw disappointment run through Will. Ory had failed him. He wouldn't make it out alive. Their journey would end bloodied, still within reach of the River Road. But Ory wasn't going to die without doing the right thing. Without telling him everything.

"You were right, Will."

"Sir?"

"You were right about me. I was never here for you."

Will nodded his head in confirmation of what he had believed. But he held nothing against Ory, there was forgiveness in his eyes. He sat back, and did the best thing that a friend could do. He listened.

"All my life, I lived in fear of what my father did and what people thought I could become. And my mother, I just wanted to make the memories of her death go away so the pain would be gone. But it's the only thing I could seem to remember. So much so, that it was all that I could see at times. I wanted so much to understand what my father did. The only memory I have of him is holding my dead mother and his last words to me. The rest are just flashes and whispers. When I saw you in that barn, Will, you held that dead man just the way my father held my mother. Then the memory of her death went away and you replaced it. It was almost identical. When I saw you, I saw a second chance. I saw a way to understand. But, I guess hope doesn't come as easy as I thought it would. Because even now as I sit before you, at the end of our road, all I see is death, and nothing more."

Will let him sit and made sure there was nothing left for Ory to say, and then spoke. "You know something Millie asked me? She asked, 'Are you the one who's going to sit around waiting for hope, Will, or are you going to be the one who brings it?' She asked me that the evening before we left."

Ory looked up recalling the very same words, on the very same night.

Will continued, "I didn't know what the hell that meant. But I've been wondering if, a lot of times, it's not what she said that mattered, but what I took from it. Maybe it's sitting in me somewhere doing something. I don't know what. Maybe nothing. I feel like I've only been worried about myself."

Ory felt the exact same way. A road that Millie thought should be paved with hope was really lined with selfishness. It would seem that had been the way for them. Taking a journey that served themselves. There was something else, however, that they both had overlooked. Something that fueled them, but they never realized. Until then, when Ory, whose heart seemed to breathe, feeling safer, could finally give a name to the thing that drove him.

"No, you haven't."

"What?"

"You haven't done just for yourself. I can prove it."

"You can?"

"Me."

"How are you proof?"

"Because you are the only thing that gives me hope in life. Since I've been with you, I've had hope that maybe things aren't as bad as they had seemed. That there is good in my life. Like I can change the world. And I hoped…my past."

Ory looked into Will's eyes with a thousand apologies. For all the things he didn't see and those he was still blind to. He promised himself he wouldn't hold his eyes shut, but would try to keep them open, especially when the world taught him not to see.

"You're a good man, sir."

"You, too. Ory."

Hope. If anything could keep them alive, it would be that. If not, it would be a worthy state to die in.

CAUGHT BY THE FIRE

Night had fallen on the town of the red dirt road. The saloon was empty for reasons other than just its broken window. No one was in the streets. The inn itself seemed desolate. The Conductor, along with Bernice and CJ, came to the front hall, about to exit. The Conductor said, "Let's try to go quickly."

CJ added, "We'll need to clear out tonight. I'm sure the marshal is on his way by now."

"Bernice and I will go first. You watch to see if we're followed."

The Conductor and Bernice grabbed their bags and left the inn. CJ watched as they made their way to their horses. He saw no one. They stood in the shadows loading their things. From behind, CJ heard a noise, he turned drawing his gun, but saw no one. He looked for a moment to make sure he didn't miss anything, then looked back to his friends outside. They were gone. CJ burst from the inn and out to the road. There was no one. Anywhere. The street was empty again. All that remained were their horses, loaded up and packed full, with no one to ride.

Not far from the inn and not far from the barn, in the woods next to a fire sat Lezin. His men lurked in the shadows around him, keeping watch. His eyes mirrored the flames. He thought to the distant past, and on the one he loved and lost, knowing he was getting closer to feeling some sort of revenge.

Next to Lezin was a body with a bag over its head, arms bound behind its back. He kicked it to make sure it was still breathing. The body gently moved, like a beaten animal, then settled back into stillness.

Footsteps were coming from the dark and the Bertran boys appeared. Jean said, "They were there, just like you said."

They threw the Conductor and Bernice on the ground by the fire.

"Good evening, Mr. Sherman. Ms. Bernice."

The two looked around. They saw the Bertran boys behind them, two dark shadows floating around in the woods, and Lezin right in front of them, sitting back, enjoying the warm light from the fire.

"Lovely town."

Bernice noticed the body on the ground next to him and the hands tied behind its back. Black hands. Bernice went cold, first from the thought of Will bound in front of her, then of Ory, because if Will was there, where was he? Lezin saw Bernice's fright and assured her, "Oh, now, don't get nervous. It's not who you think."

Lezin grabbed the bag from the body's head and pulled it off. It was Johnny. His plan had failed. The dust from their chase he thought he could find cover in eventually settled, leaving him naked in the night.

"Caught this one not far back. We thought it was our boy Will. Have to say, we were pretty disappointed. But we'll make the best of him."

Lezin smiled and patted Johnny on the back, like a friend sitting next to him around the fire. He then reached behind him and grabbed Johnny's guitar. They had picked it up when they caught him. Lezin put it down in front of Johnny and unbound his hands.

"Why don't you play for our guests?"

Johnny rubbed his wrists, feeling the blood flow back into his hands. He picked up the guitar and looked at all the white faces around him.

Lezin encouraged him, "Go on."

Johnny carefully started to strum and they all sat and listened next to the crackle of the fire. Lezin closed his eyes and tilted his head back.

"A beautiful sound."

As each second went by and Lezin said nothing, with them just sitting in the night listening to this music,

Bernice realized, as Ory did, these men weren't looking to take him home.

Lezin asked, "So, have you all seen them?"

"No."

"So, no idea where he might be?"

"No."

Lezin's face, like it did back with CJ in the city, went soft and sincere. "Listen, we just want to make sure they don't harm anyone else and bring them back to the River Road."

"Alive, right?"

"Of course."

Bernice lowered her head and nodded. Lezin enjoyed seeing her succumb to his ploy. It was going to be easier than he thought. Bernice, as if revealing secret information, "Well, in that case, they're not here anymore."

"They're not?"

"No. They said they were sorry and that they were going home to turn themselves in."

Lezin's face went hard and venom returned to his eyes.

"Is that so?"

"Yes."

"Careful, girl. I'd hate for anything to happen to that pretty face."

"As long as you don't do anything worse than that hideous thing on yours."

It wasn't hard for Lezin to hold back his urge to choke Bernice and bury her face in the coals of the fire. He remained calm, until Jacques spoke while gesturing to Jean and Oak. "Yeah, Lezin, the boys and I were wondering, where did you get that?"

Grabbing Jacques by the throat, Lezin pinned him against a tree, his feet dangling just above the ground. Johnny stopped strumming, but Lezin turned to him. "Did I tell you to stop?"

As Johnny started to play again, Lezin slid the barrel of his gun into Jacques' mouth and pressed it against his throat, choking him. Lezin came in close, whispering to him, "Do you love anything, boy?"

Jacques, trying to breath, nodded his head yes.

"Well, imagine that was all you lived for and I took it away."

Lezin pulled the gun back just a little, then moved the end and pressed it against the inside of his cheek. "Now imagine I burned a hole in your cheek reminding you everyday about it."

Lezin threw Jacques to the ground at the Bertran boys' feet. Lezin looked at them all around him. He suddenly felt insecure.

"We're going to see real quick how honest our company is."

He looked over to Johnny who was still on the ground, playing as commanded.

"Pick that nigger up." The two men came from the shadows and grabbed Johnny, his guitar fell to the ground. Lezin went over to Bernice and knelt down next to her.

"I am sure you all are now aware that Johnny here is a mighty talented individual. I've listened to him many times." Turning his back to his men, "Tie his hand down."

One servant grabbed Johnny's wrist.

"No," Lezin ordered. "The other hand."

Johnny's face looked up to Lezin. He loved both of his hands. He wouldn't want anything to happen to either of them. But this hand they tied down was the one used to make chords on the guitar. The one he absolutely could not do without. Which was why Lezin choose it. They tied one end of a rope around his wrist and the other around the trunk of a tree. The two minions then grabbed him from behind, pulling Johnny's arm and the rope taught.

Lezin came up next to him. "A man that good has to have dreams of another life. Am I right?"

Johnny didn't know what terrified him more, the flames he saw in Lezin's eyes or the whip that he pulled from under his jacket that fell to the ground. Lezin walked away from him, stopped, and turned around taking aim at Johnny's hand. Lezin said, over his shoulder to Bernice, "Whenever you're ready, you can speak up."

The whip flew back, then bounced forward, cracking into the night. Johnny was a strong man, but unlike Will, his screams would not be held.

THE DEATH OF DREAMS

Ory and Will had not moved from their spots in the center of the barn. They sat waiting for their friends to come from the inn, unaware of the danger that had befallen them. Ory knew they should have been there by now, but they couldn't leave.

CJ broke through the door. "Ory."

Ory and Will jumped up.

"Where's everyone else?"

"They got them."

"How?"

"Pulled right out of the shadows. I never saw them. He'll be coming. He'll find a way to make them talk."

Ory picked up the Colts from the ground and strapped them on. He looked at Will. Ory didn't want to leave him, but he would, even if it was to save a future that couldn't exist.

"I have to go for her."

247

Before there was any debate, another body came falling in and Ory drew his Colt. The body stumbled across the floor, saw Will, swayed left and right and landed into Will's arms.

"Johnny?"

Johnny's clothes were full of blood. He leaned in close to Will's chest, breathing hard.

"What are you doing here?"

"You said it. It was going to get me in trouble."

Johnny had one of his hands under his own arm. Blood was now spilling onto Will's clothes. Johnny looked at Ory and smiled. "I guess this means you won't be paying me for playing the guitar, Master Ory. I was good, too. Real good."

"You are good."

"We need to help him."

"No, I'm fine…fine." He shook his head and his eyes rolled back. "He's out there."

"Who did this to you?"

"Not a man. There's fire in his eyes."

Johnny lifted his bloody hand up to Will's face and ran his finger along his chin, making a blood trail on Will's face right where Lezin had his scar. Johnny's other hand fell to the side. What was left of it. It was just a bloody stump that had been whipped away.

"He wants me to send a message."

"What message?"

"We need to talk…son."

He took a deep breath, enjoying the feeling of air the best he could, then fell over dead, his empty eyes staring.

They were out there, and they were coming. CJ could be blamed for all of this. Truth is, it was destined to happen eventually. But that's not how CJ saw it. He looked out through the window then back to Ory and Will, who were still sitting over Johnny's body.

"This is my fault."

"CJ, not now. You can make it up to us by helping."

CJ looked out the window again, then back to Ory. He truly was sorry for all that he had done.

"You're right."

CJ ran out of the barn, Ory tried to grab him, but it was too late. CJ walked out into the open, toward the edge of darkness, waving his hands, signaling for anyone to approach. He focused hard on the black abyss in front of him but saw nothing.

"It's all okay. I just talked to them."

The Bertran boys slowly emerged. Jean came running to him, gun drawn.

"They in there?"

"Yes. And they are ready to come out."

"Perfect. Bring them out. I can't wait to see them bleed."

"I know."

He pulled out his gun, pressed it against Jacques' chest, and pulled the trigger. As his body ripped open, CJ tried to turn the gun on Jean. Before he could get to him,

Jean grabbed the gun and tried to shoot CJ with his, but CJ grabbed his as well. The two struggled, both holding each other's guns in their hands. Oak came from behind CJ, grabbed him by the throat and lifted him in the air. CJ let go of Jean and dropped his gun, trying to break himself free, grabbing at Oak's gargantuan hands, but it was no use. His airway was sealed. In seconds CJ's eyes turned red, and with an extra pulse from Oak's hands, there was a snap, and CJ died.

Ory and Will watched as Oak threw CJ's body to the ground.

"It's time, Will."

Ory pulled out one of the Colts and handed it to Will. Will hesitated taking the weapon, and decided not to. "I don't need that."

"They will shoot you."

Will looked back out to Jean and Oak, standing there waiting for them. "No. They won't."

Ory stared at him for a moment then nodded his head. "Okay. They're all yours."

Ory looked around for the best way out. His attention drew toward the other side as a faint scream was heard. A strange scream. Ory couldn't tell if it was Bernice or a man in the dark, holding Bernice's bound wrists, screaming wild into the night, finding enjoyment in it.

"I'll go out to the side. He's got to be out there somewhere."

Stopping him, "Ory."

Will held his hand out for Ory to shake it. Ory reached to receive it.

Will said, "I… No words seem like the right ones."

"I know what you mean."

They separated toward danger. Will walked out of the barn the same way CJ had gone. He crept out into the open, looking into the black for the Bertrans, but they were gone. He stood under the moonlight. Will saw lightning strike and he looked up to the sky as clouds rolled in, covering the moon. Then the thunder crashed and out came the Bertrans.

"There you are. There. You. Are." Jean was holding his gun to Will, looking around frantically. "Where's Ory?"

"Looking for someone."

"I bet."

He continued to look around, scanning left and right, thinking Ory would jump out at him at any moment. Oak came right up to Will. Will tilted his head back to see Oak's face, the rain hit him in the eyes.

"Mighty brave of you coming out here, all alone, with nothing."

"Oh, I got something."

Will took a step back from Oak, put up his bare knuckles and started to circle him.

"Oh, ain't that cute. He wants a fighting chance."

Oak smiled, rolling up his sleeves and cracking his knuckles, while licking the lips of his drooling face.

251

"What do you say, Oak? How about you give him one last round? And make it a good one."

They circled each other for a moment, rain saturating their soaking bodies, then Will jabbed, hitting Oak in the face. Oak's head barely moved. Oak took a swing but Will ducked, delivering two more jabs and one strong hook to his face. Oak's head jerked back. When he turned back to Will, his lip was bleeding.

"He's feisty, huh, Oak?"

Jean continued to watch and enjoy the show, just like those days back in the barn on the River Road. Will knew Jean wouldn't refuse the opportunity to see this. Oak took a lunging step forward, grabbing Will by the shirt with one hand and with the other, crushed it into Will's face. Will flew to the ground and slid in the water. Oak smiled. Will lay in the water. He picked his head up and shook it. Oak motioned for Will to get up and said in a slow, deep voice, "Come on, baby nigger."

Will got up, picking up his fists and moved in again. They circled. Will moved in close and got in a small jab, then swung wide but Oak caught his arm and punched him in the stomach. Will fell to the ground but was pulled back up like a puppet on a string. Oak gave a couple more hits to Will's chest, then let him fall to the ground. His body hit like a sack in the water.

"That's it, Oak."

Will was on his back. He coughed hard and blood came from his mouth and down the side of his face. The rain slowed and the clouds cleared. Will looked up to the stars through the drizzle. A sensation came over him. He thought to himself, this situation that he was in, as deadly as it was, he was here by choice, and he could either choose to get up or choose to die. This was the choice of a free man. The rain started up again, harder than before, and the clouds moved back in. Will stood up but didn't raise his hands. Oak and Jean came over to him. Oak grabbed his shoulders from behind and held him facing Jean.

Jean got right in Will's face. "Let this be your last lesson. Don't ever try fighting a white man."

Will slammed his head into Jean's nose, feeling millions of cracks and parts of bone shattering as they made contact, and then Jean fell unconscious to the mud. Will slipped through, underneath Oaks arms, behind him, punching twice, hard, just underneath his ribs. Oak screamed and turned around swinging, but Will dodged and danced around him, beating his fists along Oak's torso like a drum. Will jumped back. Oak squared off with Will, who didn't hesitate and launched his fist right between Oak's eyes. And then another. And another. And Oak began to sway. Will waited for Oak to stop rocking, then, crack, Will punched Oak so hard he dislocated his jaw and it was left hanging by skin and tissue. He walked up to Oak, kicked his knee, cracking it, bending it backwards, forcing Oak to collapse to his level, and Will grabbed his huge head, spun it hard, and broke his neck.

Will stood in the rain over the bodies of a giant and a pawn.

Ory walked out the other side of the barn. The rain was coming down, and standing out there waiting for him was Lezin, holding Bernice and the Conductor out in front of him, both with rags tied across their mouths. The Conductor's face was bloody and beaten, a result of withholding information.

"Lezin."

"Sorry we have to meet again like this. I didn't want you to do anything rash. I just want civilized talk."

"We'll talk, if you let them go."

Lezin pulled out his gun and shot the Conductor in the back of the head. Blood fell to the ground as did the Conductor's dead body.

"No negotiations."

Ory dropped his head, cringing, careful not to make any more mistakes.

"Oh, come on, Ory. Don't pretend like he was the important one."

The rain water that was beginning to rise around the barn was turning red from the blood pouring from the Conductor's head.

"Look, I'll put you at ease." He threw his gun away and threw Bernice to the ground. "See. Everything is fine."

Ory searched the darkness looking around for others but saw no one. They walked closer to each other.

"I just wanted to finish our conversation."

"Not happening."

Ory pulled out the Colt.

"Ory, you insult me."

Lezin's minions came from the shadows and knocked Ory's gun from his hand. They were quick to restrain Ory's arms and pulled them behind his back. Lezin approached Ory and punched him in the gut. Ory fell to his knees and Lezin's servants tied his hands behind his back. Lezin punched him in the face. In the distance, Bernice, hands bound, made a charge for them, but it was worthless without the use of her arms and Lezin's minions simply grabbed her, dragging her away.

"Just give us a minute, boys."

"You're not here for Will are you?"

"No, sir." Lezin kicked Ory in the face. "Now. We will finish our conversation. The one you so rudely ended." He brought Ory back up to his knees, sitting him upright. "Like they say, the sins of the father…"

Lezin punched his target and Ory fell back into the sludge around him. Lezin picked him up again. Blood and mud covered Ory's face. Lezin pulled back for another hit, but stopped when Ory said, "I remember you."

"You do?"

"Yes. My parents fought over you. Whatever you and my mother had, it's in the past."

"Oh, no. It's carried well into the present and it's kneeling right in front of me."

Lezin punched him and when his head slowly rolled back forward, Ory said, "I'm sorry."

"You're sorry?" Lezin slid in, kneeled with Ory, face to face, holding himself back from choking him. "Sorry? Do you know what it's like to have love ripped out of you? To be left lifeless and cold?"

"Yes. I do."

Ory's fear of Lezin had left him. He had learned so much that day, about his past, and about himself. And he chose to see Lezin for what he really was. A man not much different than Ory. He was a man who had something taken from him. Ory could understand that. They mourn the loss of the same thing.

"You don't know what I had. It's not the same."

"It is."

"It's not. I just want to let you know, Ory, this doesn't stop with you. No, no, no. After this, your Titaunt is going to need someone." Lezin pulled from under his shirt the silver magnolia, the necklace he had taken from Titaunt. "And your sister, how old is she now? Far too young not to have a father figure in her life. Don't worry. I'll take care them. Look at me, I promise you, they'll be safe. I can do it. They don't look like him. They look like your mother. That'll keep them safe."

"You don't have to do this. You can let it go."

"There's no letting go. This is how it was supposed to be. Understand me, son. I told her I would help raise you. That I could bring you up to be a good man. You, me, your sister, we were going to be happy. But he wasn't going to let it happen. Like I told you before, I tried to warn her. But it was too late."

"How did you know he was going to kill her?"

"He was killing her everyday. Inside. She just couldn't see it."

"She couldn't see it?"

"No, no, I tried. I tried to show her, but she wouldn't listen. And one day I just couldn't take it anymore."

"Take what?"

"That she didn't love me."

At first Ory thought that he heard Lezin wrong, but he didn't. He knew by the churning that began.

"It had to be done. I was dying without her. She was, too, I know she was. I had to relieve her pain. She was sick. She lost it, and grabbed my knife and cut my face." He felt his scar. "That assured me it had to be done. I was going to make it look like a suicide. But your father got home and I hid. He came in and found her. He thought she had killed herself." Lezin started to laugh, "So, he picked up the knife in disbelief. It was perfect. But then, he just sat there. He didn't move. He didn't cry. He didn't yell. He did nothing. That's what he thought love was. You see?"

"You're lying. You're crazy."

"I would have torn the world apart."

"My father would have said something."

"Who knows what he was thinking? Good thing he died, though. I wouldn't have been able to look at his face. The one who took her from me. He did this, you know?"

Mud and blood still covered Ory's face, in shock, frozen in disbelief.

"I took it upon myself to take a vow of silence. And that would be my penance, to have to live with it, and I was doing well, too. But ever since you have been back, my mind has been spinning. God, you look just like him. He's mocking me from the grave. But it's okay. We are going to stop that right now."

Lezin pulled from behind his coat his long whip and it came splashing down into the water below. He pointed to Ory with the whip. "I didn't mean to kill your father. I just want to make that clear. Not that I wouldn't have or didn't want to, it just was not my intention." Letting out a deep breath, "Its been wonderful to finally say this to someone."

Lezin stood and took a few steps back from Ory and got his whip ready to strike. He wanted to see Ory's eyes, but they were facing the ground, defeated. Destroyed. Lezin smiled enjoying the last few seconds of the man that haunted his dreams. The rain's reflection was caught in his eyes, and what light was trapped in them flickered like flames. Lezin closed them, as if he felt a warmth on his face. He took a slow breath and said to Ory, "We would have made a good family."

Ory looked up to Lezin with his lost red eyes, his memories churning faster than ever, and as Lezin pulled his whip back, Ory heard a gunshot. Will was standing right behind one of Lezin's minions and had put a gun to his head, adding another soul to their cursed names. Bernice fell and the other servant tackled Will to the ground.

Lezin turned back to Ory and watched his arms slowly fall from behind him and out in front, wrists cut free by the knife Ory had in his hand, the one that once cut Will's palm. Lezin looked on and Ory didn't move. He just knelt there, still.

"Son?"

Ory grabbed his watch and opened it. The frozen hands of time appeared to shake. As he looked down onto his mother's portrait, a drop of blood hung from Ory's cheek. It fell, splashing on the image below. Her cloudy black and white face now covered in red. Ory saw Will again, holding the body in front of the bed and then his old memory returned and he saw his father holding his mother, but it was different. He saw deep into his father's eyes and saw the innocence that he knew in Will. An innocent man, shot beyond the ability to greave, forced into a world of the impossible, with a woman in his arms that he had loved and couldn't live without. Ory stood, among the mud and the blood, looking up to the dragon.

Lezin looked at the man before him and that fear he had felt that day with him on the River Road had returned, but with it came that face from the past, challenging him to finish what he had started.

"As fate would have it. Father versus son. Part of me feared you all those years ago. I saw an older you standing in my dreams, knowing the truth. But it was only a dream. And in reality, you are but the remnants of two creatures that I have released from this hell. I had to do it. And with you, he'll be erased, lingering here no more."

"You should have killed me back on the River Road. You should have told me all that in hell."

Lezin cracked his whip to the side of him and across the flooded ground, exploding on its surface, sending a mist about them, raindrops retreating back to the sky. The rain faded away. Their eyes beamed, flames in Lezin's and the sharp lunar light shining in Ory's. Then Lezin flipped the whip back and flung it forward, but Ory stepped in throwing his arm in front, allowing the whip to wrap around it. Lezin tried to pull it back but couldn't. Blood ran down Ory's forearm. Stuck, both unable to pull away, they charged, tackling each other in the water. Ory stood Lezin up and punched him in the stomach. Lezin fell to his knees and Ory grabbed the necklace from around his neck, ripping it off. "This doesn't belong to you."

Ory punched him again. Lezin popped back up, grabbing Ory and driving him several feet, slamming him onto the flooded ground, sliding in the mud.

Will, who had been wrestling with the other minion, managed to get on top of him. The servant's stomach was on the ground and Will held his face in the mud, underwater. His legs kicked and his arms tried to grab Will, but they all failed, and he died.

Will went to Bernice, took off her gag and untied her hands. "Are you okay?"

"Yes. We have to help him."

Lezin was standing behind Ory with his arm around his neck, choking him. Ory was losing consciousness as Will jumped onto the dragon's back, attempting to choke him. Will held tight as the beast jumped and bucked, trying to throw him off. Lezin spun Will around, moving to the barn wall, and smashed Will into it. And smashed. And smashed again. The barn wall caved in as Lezin broke through it with Will's body. Will rolled on the ground, arms wrapped across his chest, holding the back of his ribs, hardly moving. Lezin walked back out, found his gun on the ground and approached Ory. Bernice jumped in front of him, standing in his way. But Lezin didn't hesitate, said nothing, and punched Bernice out of the way. At that moment, Ory came back to and sprung forward to Lezin, but slammed into Lezin's gun pressing against his head. Ory put his hands up.

Lezin caught his breath. "This is getting out of hand."

Jean came running from the other side of the barn. "The marshal." His skeleton-like nose was oozing blood, spilling down his shirt. He breathed hard through his mouth. "We don't have time."

"Calm down."

"No. We have to kill these two before it's too late."

Jean was in the full bent of his rage. He was all that was left of his family, and he was looking to get the revenge that was due to him. Biting hard on his bottom lip, he raised his gun to Ory's heart, and almost had him. But Jean knew nothing of the man who led him there. Nothing of the man next to him. Lezin would never let that happen. He would not lose his prize, not to him, or anyone. Before Jean could pull the trigger, his heart exploded as a bullet ripped through his chest, and his body splashed in the flooded water at Ory's feet. A blink and one would have missed it. It was as if Lezin's gun never moved. Then it was right back, pressing hard against Ory's head.

"I said, calm down."

In the distance, dozens of horses appeared. The marshal had arrived. Bernice stood to confirm who was coming. Ory closed his eyes and exhaled, holding a bittersweet smile. He looked at Lezin. The dragon would fail. Ory would be caught, and not murdered in the shadows.

Lezin squinted, observing the relief he saw in the two of them, a chance for an ending not made by him. Lezin smiled. "Looks like this is the end, Ory." Lezin tilted his head, then turned to Bernice and pointed the gun at her. "You know what? I don't think I'm ready. Ory, you are going to leave with me and you're going to run. If you don't move right now, she dies."

Bernice was ready to call his bluff, but not Ory. He knew what happened to him if he left with Lezin alone and unarmed. He knew what came to Will if he was caught by the marshal. But neither of those things mattered in that moment, when it was Bernice's life that was dancing with death. Then the moon was gone from Ory's eyes, and both men fell into the darkness, vanishing into the woods.

Bernice had little time to think, the marshal was upon them. She ran to Will inside the barn. She took him by the collar. "Will, get up. We have to run. Get up."

He staggered to his feet and they left the barn, but it was too late. The marshal would catch them before the woods. Bernice looked around at what little options she had left, and saw the Colts on the ground. She grabbed them, hurrying to dress Will in them.

"What are you doing?"

"Take me hostage."

"What?"

"Put the gun to my head." Bernice threw herself onto Will's chest, putting Will's arm around her neck. "Help!"

Will saw exactly what she was doing and pulled the Colt out, pressing it to her head, slowly backing away toward the woods. The marshal and his men approached, guns drawn aiming at Will.

"Let her go, boy."

"No, sir. Don't you come any closer."

Dozens of men were lined up in front of them, dozens of guns pointed at Will's head, many of the men already squeezing their triggers halfway in. The marshal gaged the standoff, looking at Will and Bernice, considering the shot. He held his hand up, signaling to his men to back off and lower their weapons. Will slowly backed away. Soon, Will and Bernice could no longer be seen, hidden in the shadows of the woods, and they ran. They got a good distance before Bernice stopped. Torches lit up in the distance behind them.

"Will, I'm going back. I'll tell the marshal I escaped. It'll buy you some time."

Will said nothing. He just stared at her. She put her hands on his face and kissed him, and looked at him as if it was the last time. The first time.

"I…I'm sorry."

Will was still frozen, saying nothing. Bernice didn't know why she did it. Neither did Will. She only did what she wanted to do. And that's what it was in that moment. A touch and a kiss. A connection.

"Find him, please."

And then, Bernice was gone.

Will stood between two deadly forces. Alone. He felt an urge, as he did back in Ory's home, awaiting the dawn to light Henri Bertran's death. Once again, he felt that temptation to run. To leave Ory to face the shadow. To go and face his own. He could either continue deep into the swamp, into the dragon's cave, or back out into the light, to the world that wanted his blood. Either way, he thought, *Dead men.*

THE FORGOTTEN PLACES OF THIS LAND

Ory assumed they were all that remained of the chase. The Bertrans and the shadow's minions were all gone. And Will, too, captured by the marshal, sure to be dead. All those involved had dwindled to two. They came deep into the woods and arrived at the edge of the swamp, back to the dragon's cave, and as they did, Lezin put Ory to his knees, binding his wrists behind him. Lezin stood back, staring at Ory, waiting, as if he knew what was coming. Slowly the white fog crept in, while whispers were carried on the wind. The two listened as this white spirit surrounded them. They both just listened. Ory could feel it on his skin, crawling like a cold spider down his arm. He breathed, feeling it coat his lungs. It was here. It had finally come.

Lezin holstered his gun.

"Well, that didn't turn out as we had hoped." Lezin laughed and looked to Ory thinking he'd find that amusing. He didn't. When his laugh subsided, Lezin approached Ory, squatting down in front of him. "I'm sorry, son."

Ory didn't respond. His fog-consumed body had no fight left in him, there was no cause to speak.

"What happens next, I take much delight in. My job. The marshal would have me take you back. But I see that in your current state that might not be the charitable deed. And I am feeling charitable."

Ory continued to kneel. Dead body. Dead eyes. As if his own spirit had gone the way with Will and just his body remained.

"We could journey back to the River Road, and all those days you could think about your failure. You could think about what you have waiting for you there. Or, you take my charitable offering, and you can meet it here. Just you and me. No more waiting."

No more waiting. Ory's eyes moved to Lezin. That he could understand. That Will could understand. And he didn't want to wait any longer. His head nodded and Lezin's did, too.

"Good choice. You're actually the first to take that offer, to be honest. But before we do this, tell me...do you think I could have made a good father?"

Ory didn't know what a good father was anymore. He didn't know what memories to trust. Which ones were real. His mind had been abused and manipulated his whole life. But he trusted that this thing before him killed

267

his father. And it didn't take a memory to convince himself that he didn't want to be the dragon. He never became him. It is what the River Road wanted to turn him into. Lezin fixed Ory's hair a bit, making it neater, as neat as possible when soaked in rain, and mud and blood.

"I could have. Ah, well."

Lezin stood up and made a slight click in his mouth and his black steed emerged from the darkness. He took out his whip and grabbed a rope from the saddle, and tied them together. He walked behind Ory, who never moved, never even flinched, as Lezin slowly wrapped the whip around his neck. He threw the rope over a tree branch above him and tied the other end to his horse. Still, Ory knelt, frozen once more. Lezin wondered for a moment. He had never seen a man do that before. Then he thought, *No, wait. I have.* And he had. About a decade before.

"Let's go."

Lezin walked back with his horse. The rope tightened. The whip tightened. And Ory began to rise. First his head and chest. Then his legs, knees leaving the ground. Slowly. He then stood for the last time. His heels went up, and his toes kissed the ground and left it. He did not struggle. The white fog swirled around him while Lezin looked upon his victory, as the only one who would remain. But as Ory's eyes closed, the rope released and it burned the bark, running hard and fast across it, and Ory's body came crashing to the ground.

From the other side of Lezin's black steed came the Colt, held by Will, aiming at Lezin. Ory coughed as his blurry vision came into focus and he saw that his friend had escaped, was alive, and had come for him. Each man was cautious, no sudden movements, every step was slow and calculated. Will walked around the horse holding the gun steady on Lezin. Ory saw Lezin's gun holstered, not far for Lezin to grab, having the ability to easily out draw a man so new to firearms.

"You sure you know how to use that thing?"

Both Ory and Lezin thought of the holstered gun, but not Will. Will thought only of the gun in his hand, the one Ory showed him how to use, the one he was warned with, warned of the ones after them, those who did not seek justice and only revenge and darkness, that if he ever had to use it, to use it, never hesitating. Will fired a shot hitting Lezin in the shoulder, twisting him around and to his knees.

"You God damn nigger."

Will fired again, hitting him in the other shoulder, taking away the use of his arms. Ory got up as Lezin rolled and crawled, dragging himself to the tree, and leaned his back against it.

Ory walked over to Will. "So, I guess we're even."

Will handed the Colt to Ory and they both fell to the ground exhausted. They leaned their backs together, both supporting the other. And then again, as the day Ory rode back onto the River Road, they were overcome by an ease, the comfort felt by the campfire in the swamp among memories told, the same sense of hope brought to them in their meeting yesterday on the red dirt road, that compassion that grew each day as they understood the other more. And there they sat. Mirrored. As one. The fog became illuminated as the moonlight joined them, finding its place in both their eyes.

They never looked at the dragon who bled only feet away. Lezin leaned his head back to the tree trying to escape the moon's light, hoping for a shadow. He growled, ground his teeth, and tried to suppress the pain coming from the holes Will put in him. As he looked back to the two of them, he searched for whatever menace was left in him. "You two are dead. I promise you."

They didn't move. They remained still and Will said, "I'm sorry, sir. But you are already looking at dead men."

The fire inside Lezin began to fade, and he now felt like those he chased all these years on the River Road, consumed by fear.

"So, what? You're going to bring me to the marshal? To Cogan? Tell them the truth? See me hanged? Hell, maybe we'll hang together."

"No."

The two of them stood up as if lifted by the fog and Ory casually floated toward Lezin and squatted down in front of him.

"I'm feeling charitable."

The flames in Lezin's eyes tried to roar up at what he feared was to come, but he could do nothing, facing a bullet and bleeding dry.

"Will, would you tie that rope, please?"

Will, with the same indifference, went to the rope he had untied while Ory was being hanged, and tied the whip back to it.

"No. No, Ory. Not like this."

"Tie the whip around his neck."

Lezin squirmed, unable to move his arms, and Will dragged him from the tree, sitting him up neatly as if he were stacking cane back on the plantation. He wrapped the whip around his neck.

"Before we do this, ask me... Ask me not to do it."

"Ory, please."

"Ask me to be your son."

"Let me be a father to you."

Ory came close to Lezin as that fiery blood dripped from the dragon's body and onto the ground. All he could see were Ory's eyes. The eyes of his mother. And Ory requested one last thing, wanting the truth.

"Tell me you loved my mother."

"Everyday she lived. I wanted a life with her."

"So did I."

Ory stood and backed away.

"You won't do it."

"You're right. I won't."

From Will's mouth came the identical click made from Lezin's earlier, and the horse started to move. Will left it and stood next to Ory.

"Ory. You don't want to do this. There is still more you don't know." The rope tightened and Lezin was pulled up to standing. "All those fights your parents had, the ones you remembered. It wasn't all about me, Ory. There's so much I can tell you."

"I'm letting it go. The past is dead. And so are you."

Lezin's body left the ground, he jerked back and forth a moment trying to break free, then became still. Will made another click from his mouth, stopping the horse. It held steady. Lezin looked down to them. Ory stared into the dragon's eyes, those flames still lingering, but then like a firestorm rolling around inside. The fire began to dwindle, and as Lezin looked into Ory's eyes, he saw the woman he loved, the woman he killed, the son she had created, the father that lived in him. He thought, *They were right. He is just like his father.* The flames in his eyes turned to embers, and went black. The whispers on the wind seemed to turn to screams, and Ory and Will watched as the white spirit floated around the body in the night air, then passed through him, dragging his soul deep into the swamp to be forgotten forever.

Will and Ory stood below the hanging corpse. The dragon was slain and would hunt them no more.

"It seems our curse still lingers."

"Yes. But this one doesn't count."

As they stood, a small band of rain came through, showering them through the trees. Ory continued to watch the hollowed remains as the rain washed the blood clean from Ory's face, the mud dissolved clear from his hair. He pulled the watch from his pocket, revealing to the rain the blood splattered portrait. Her face, too, was washed clean. And then the rain was gone again.

There is no telling how long they would have stayed there, as if to guard the dead body, being sure to see it decay. But torches began to appear around them, coming into sight from the shadows, approaching them. So the body was left, hanged by the dragon's own design, remaining in the darkness that it lived, owned now by the swamp and the creatures that dwelled within it.

BURNING FOR FREEDOM

The two of them ran blindly in the darkness, branches cutting their faces as they pushed through, the torches gaining on them. They hoped that they could outrun them, hide just for a day, but Ory noticed that the torches following them were diverting them back to the town of the red dirt road.

"They're flushing us out Will. We'll be surrounded soon."

The trees thinned and they saw torches ahead of them, but that didn't stop them. They kept running hard, as if they could break through anything in their way. As they came out of the woods, they were easily spotted by the marshal and his men. Bernice stood among them, unharmed and out of the way. She saw Ory and Will just as the marshal did and they both screamed at the same time.

"Ory."

"Hold it."

Ory and Will stopped at the sight of long barrels pointed at them, but the barn was not far from where they were, and in a last desperate attempt to survive, they darted for it. Gunshots rang out, bullets flying past them, trying to pierce their bouncing bodies in the dark, and almost all missed, save for one that hit Ory in the back of the thigh, sending him to the ground. Will grabbed him, threw Ory's arm over his shoulder and dragged him into the barn. They fell through the entrance to the barn that Will's body made when it smashed through earlier. Their bodies came crashing down and they crawled to safety.

Ory looked down to his bleeding leg, telling himself it was just a nick, but he knew it wasn't. It was torn open and deep. No more running. He wrapped his leg and tightened it with a knot.

"I think we should just hole up here for a while."

The window to the barn shattered as one of the torches came flying in. One of the doors was kicked opened and another torch flew in. Then one through the entrance they fell from. Then another, and another, until they burned the hay and the wood, setting flames all around them.

Men emerged from the darkness of the woods and into the moonlight holding their torches. The marshal and his officers were surrounding the barn, their arms up, shielding their eyes from the growing flames. Bernice ran to the marshal. "You have to get them out of there."

"I can't risk the lives of my men to pull out a killer. They can come out or they burn."

A couple of officers grabbed Bernice and pulled her to safety.

"Ory. Come on out. But know, we will shoot you if you give us cause."

Ory looked out to them through the window, ducking under the growing flames, catching sight of what was waiting for them outside. He turned back to Will who sat alone in the only area that had not yet been reached by the flames.

Ory said, "I guess we better get moving."

"No. I think this is where we say goodbye."

"Tired of running?"

"No. Tired of living."

"So, I guess it's over either way."

"I am not going to go back there so they can kill me the way they want."

"Will, burning is a hell of a way to go."

"That may be, but it sure beats going back." Will pulled out the other Colt left holstered on his chest. "We had ourselves a run didn't we?"

"Yeah."

"This is the end."

"No."

"Ory... I never thought I'd ever be free. I never had any plans to run. It was you who put me on the road. Out there, in the rain, lying broken, I watched the stars and I saw them for the first time. You know what I realized? I like seeing with free eyes. It's okay to end it here. Cause I'll die free. Let me do that. Don't let the River Road cage my eyes again. Let me be free."

Ory didn't want to leave another loved one dead in his memories. But he wouldn't deny his friend his last wish. Ory trusted him, and told himself that Will knew better than he did, that Will knew where he wanted his end. But Ory would not watch it happen. Ory stood a few steps away. Looking on his friend one last time.

"I'm sorry."

"Let it go."

Ory held hard to Will's desire, and looked on him as if he was already dead, as if that bullet was only sending him on his way, to a place of freedom, to a place where no one would be after him. Ory could very well have met his end there, too. But for Ory, the journey wasn't over. Another life was still connected to his, one with an unknown history of a mother taken, and he knew he couldn't leave her behind. He wouldn't let her become like him.

Seconds later, Ory slowly came out of the door, singed by the flames around him, and the men carefully surrounded their murderer. They grabbed him and brought him away from the barn and to his knees, shackling his wrists. He was thrown to the ground, made to watch the barn burn.

Will knelt as the flames roared around him, holding the weapon he was introduced to only a few days earlier. He brought the Colt to his head, pressed the hot steal to his temple, and pulled the hammer back. He closed his eyes and held them tight, took in a deep breath, sucking in ash and heat, then roared like the flames around him, a sound that reverberated through the barn walls, as if the cracking and bursting of flaming wood was his doing. There was a crash. Will opened his eyes to see one of the beams from the barn's roof come down in the fire, breaking through the wall, making a new opening in the back, leading to the outside. A place unguarded. Will looked back out to Ory and the marshal, then to the Colt.

Ory knelt silently staring at the barn, and the marshal and his men jumped at the sound of a gunshot from within. Ory closed his eyes. Bernice knelt down next to him, but did not comfort him.

Back in the barn, Will was still alive and moving fast. He threw the Colt down on the ground and crawled under the flames, under the burning wall whose planks and beams were popping and cracking from the intense pressure of the heat. As he crawled outside and into the brush, he could see in the distance Ory kneeling, still surrounded by the marshal's men. No one saw him escape. They were all fixed on their deadly captive and the roaring flames. Will moved slowly through the brush, staying just inside the darkness, and he made his way around to the other side of the barn. He crept in, careful not to break any branches under his feet or make any noticeable movements, as he was now right next to the marshal and his men, with Ory and Bernice in the center of them.

Will searched the ground and found a small log. He picked it up, feeling its weight, gripping it low to test its ability to be swung. He came right to the edge of the light, calculating the distance between him and Ory. He took a few quick breaths as if he were about to dive underwater, gripped his club tight, and just before he plunged in, Ory's head turned. It turned right to Will. Bernice, the marshal, and the men gazed at the inferno, but Ory turned. Looking dead into Will's eyes, but seeing only darkness. Will stepped back from the edge of the light and knelt, sharing in this mirrored look. Ory wondered if he saw something. Part of him hoped that it was Will and he was alive, but he saw nothing. Will turned from Ory to the men, to the marshal and the guns, to the fire, running every possible scenario in his head, but they all ended with the same outcome, with both of them dead. He gripped his club tight, ready to smash something. Will was willing to run through dozens of men to save Ory, thirty guns at least, all while wielding a stick. He saw Ory again and they continued to look at their reflections as the flames calmed. Neither of them thought it would have ever ended like this. They had assumed, if anything, they would die together. And Will would still have it so. But then something came to him from the light in Ory's eyes,

279

as if Ory suddenly saw him there. Will remembered, Ory's request before leaving alone for the city. His request that they wouldn't fail each other. To honor their sacrifice. He saw it again, as if Ory bestowed it upon the darkness before him. A request, not as his owner, but as his friend, to go against what the River Road had taught him, and to value his own life. To run. To leave him behind. To be a dead man who saw the possibility of life and took it, and didn't run face first into his demise because he felt he owed someone. Ory and Will could only try to save each other so many times. The truth is, not everyone can be rescued, and some aren't meant to be. The decision became clear. Their luck had run out and no hope remained. Will did not want to leave Ory's eyes, but when the flames were gone and the sun rose, Will could not be there. He took one last look at Ory's face, then dropped his wooden weapon, and was gone.

Dawn was creeping in. The barn's flames dwindled as Will ran fast through the town of the red dirt road. As he came up to the town's bar, two men were outside, and a horse stood not far from them. He ran right up, jumped, flung himself through the air, over the back of the horse, into the saddle, and rode off into the night. The two men looked at each other, said nothing and continued to drink. He was never chased. He was free.

The rest remained at the northeast corner of town until the flames were out, the barn was burned, and the sun rose over the town of the red dirt road. Smoke floated from the barn's coals. The marshal gently crunched through the ashy remains with his boots. He arrived at the center, where Ory and Will last saw each other. He looked down and saw the remains of a body. One with a hole in his charred skull that a bullet blasted through, the Colts on the ground next to it. Ory would never go to check for himself, he took the marshal's word for it, and he would never know, that the body the marshal saw was Johnny's, with the hole that Will shot into his dead bones. They all mistook the body for Will's. And so the chase was over.

The marshal and his men escorted Ory, bound in chains, back home to the River Road. Caught by its long arm, and dragged back without his friend, with a new memory. Back to end his life. Back to the belly of the River Road.

THE FINAL DAYS ON THE RIVER ROAD

The river lurked along the bend as it wound around the River Road Plantation. Things were cold and quiet there, as the river was hungry, ready to feed on the return of the one it pulled back.

The marshal drove a wagon along the River Road with Ory and Bernice sitting in the back, surrounded by dozens of men. Men armed, weapons out and ready. The two didn't look at each other much, and sat in the cold silence of the road. Even the wagon wheels and the horses' hooves seemed muffled. They could see the plantation coming into view. It wouldn't be long.

Ory looked to Bernice, who still gazed away from him, her hands clasped together. Maybe praying. Maybe hoping. Ory had time for neither. He didn't even have time to process all that he had learned, but he refused to struggle with what to believe. Lies were all that Ory had dwelled on for a good part of his life. How his life ended no longer mattered to him, but with what little time there was left, he had to make sure that the life of another didn't take the same path as his.

Ory broke the silence, "There's nothing I can do."

Bernice looked up to Ory as if she had dreaded a talk like this the entire ride. A talk of the end. Ory had no power left. No ability physically to help anyone anymore. But he was not the only one who knew the truth.

Ory continued, "You have to save her."

"You'll be able to do that yourself."

"Bernice. We know what happens when this wagon stops."

"You can't say that for sure."

"Look around us." The marshal's men all kept their eyes fixed on Ory, their fingers wrapped around their triggers, waiting, possibly hoping Ory would make the slightest move. "There's no one left."

"What do you expect me to do?"

"Make sure she knows the truth. Set her free from this place."

"My father will take everything. How will they go anywhere with nothing left?"

"Then she'll grow up like I did."

Ory knew the River Road would try to blind Sidonie with its lies, shielding her from who he really was, who her family was. Sidonie was in line to become like Ory. Ruined. Hidden behind a black wall. But if she knew of

Ory's road, of the truth he revealed, she'd live with hope. She would live free from the hold of the River Road.

Bernice said, "Sidonie needs her brother."

"She won't get him."

"I need her brother."

Ory stared into her eyes and then looked away. Bernice nodded in acceptance and fell silent again, thinking only of the life she thought they would have had, now knowing that life was never possible. Not on the River Road.

She asked, "Did you ever see us being happy?"

"I did."

She thought back to the evening of their engagement party, when they stood watching the river, reunited and thinking that even in this arranged relationship they could find happiness.

"That night on the porch, looking at the moon on the river. I wanted you to kiss me."

"And I still regret not doing it."

And he wouldn't then. The wagon pulled up to the planation and stopped. The marshal got out and opened the back of the wagon, holding his hand out to Bernice. The two looked at each other. Their eyes tried to hold on as they both felt themselves already floating away. Soon Bernice took the marshal's hand. Time. If only they had more time.

Inside the plantation Cogan and the marshal were in the room near the parlor, the spot where Cogan had given Ory the Colts. He sat at his desk staring at the same guns, only now they were covered in mud, ash, and gun powder. Cogan asked the marshal, "How many?'

"Fourteen. And the slave."

Cogan brought his hand to his face, rubbing his temples. "If only I'd known what these things would have done."

Bernice came in, she didn't knock, just forced herself right in. She was back in those clothes of the plantation, clean and in a dress. Cogan got up and met her with the same force in the middle of the room.

"Don't you come in here."

"You need to listen."

"Not after what you put me and your mother through, almost getting yourself killed."

"You need to let him go."

"Not only is that impossible, but why would I do that?"

"Because I love him."

"You'll learn to love someone else. We'll find you someone. Your choice this time."

"I choose him."

"Him?"

"He's innocent."

"Fourteen, Bernice. Fourteen dead men. And a slave."

"You'll kill me."

"Understand. It is out of my hands."

Cogan retreated back behind his desk, looking out of his window to the road below. Bernice wished that he was wrong, but she knew he was right. Ory wasn't only in the hands of Cogan, but of all those who sought justice for the lives lost. He was in the hands of the River Road. And that was a force with which Cogan could not contend. She kept herself upright and asked, "How is it to be done?"

"He'll hang."

"Where?"

"Outside. For the town to see."

"You can't."

"I'm sorry."

Bernice approached her father's desk, holding back, struggling to remain in control of her tears. "Father, if you can't give me him, give me this. Do not hang him out there like his father. Please."

Cogan thought awhile, trying to envision Ory's hanging, wondering if it would satisfy his need for vengeance. He thought, *It would be fitting, seeing him hang in the mirror image of his father.*

Cogan sighed and turned to Bernice. "Alright. There will be many disappointed people, but all they really want is justice." Cogan turned to the marshal and nodded, then slowly looked back out to the road. "Satisfied?"

Bernice's sorrow was beginning to change. Her father's ease and disconnect dug inside her. His question twisted like a knife in her stomach.

"Yes."

"Good. You can leave."

On her way out, she turned to her father and asked, "What is going to happen to Ory's aunt and sister?"

That thought had already been rolling around in Cogan's mind, and it continued as he looked through the window. "Don't worry. We'll take care of them."

In the center of another room in the plantation, completely clear of furniture, Ory sat in a chair on top of a large rug. Two men stood at the door armed. Ory was back to waiting. Hoping that he would know before he died. To know she'd be safe. He had gained so much, and lost, too, but his pain stemmed from the uncertainty of what could happen to those he was leaving behind. And that's when the doors flew open.

"Ory."

"Sidonie."

She ran and jumped into his arms, Titaunt following right behind her.

"I won't let you go."

"Sugar, listen. Look what I got."

Ory pulled out his gold watch and gave it to her. He helped her press the button and the door popped open and they both looked on their mother's face, Sidonie for the first time. She looked up to him and her eyes welled up.

"It'll be like looking in a mirror."

"No, don't leave. Not again. You can't leave."

"It's okay. It's okay to cry. You are so beautiful. You have a long life ahead of you. You'll fall in love and have little girls of your own."

"But, I want you."

"And I will be there with you, every step of the way. You take care of Titaunt for me."

Titaunt knelt down next to him and held his cheek. "I knew you never should have come back here."

"But good thing I did."

He pulled from his pocket her necklace and handed it to her. "He won't harm us anymore."

"Are you sure?"

"I'm sure. When, I'm gone. Bernice will have some things to tell you. Believe them. They come from me."

Titaunt nodded. Ory turned back to Sidonie.

She said, "You promised me."

"I did. Some promises are hard to keep." Ory kissed Sidonie on the forehead and held her face. "Be my angel for me now."

Ory took one long look more, not only for himself, but so that she could take time to remember his face, to think of it when hard times came. The two men guarding Ory opened the door. It was time. He stood and walked out of the room, leaving the legacy of his family behind, collapsed in each other's arms, never to see him again.

It wasn't long before night fell. The river seemed eager. Ory came out of the doors of the planation and onto the porch. Cogan stood there waiting, leaning against one of the huge columns, looking out to the river. The men brought Ory to him. Cogan wouldn't look at Ory when he said, "Like father, like son. They all said it, but I never listened."

Cogan turned, grabbing Ory with his eyes, wishing he could hang him himself.

"At the request of my daughter I am doing this. Give me one reason to bring you out to the road in front of everyone, and I will."

Ory made no response.

"I gave you everything. Even my daughter. And you tried to destroy that. And you made a good attempt. I want you to know, all the damage and humiliation you caused me... Your death does not pay the debts of those crimes."

Cogan came in close and whispered in his ear. "When you are gone, do you think there's nothing left to take? There is. Your aunt. Your sister. I am going to take everything from them. When you are gone, the land and all you own will go to me. Don't think I can't make that happen. And when they are left poor and stripped to nothing, it will be my life's mission to make sure that no one forgets who they are, and the cursed name that they bear."

Cogan stood back from Ory. He had hoped to get a rise out of him but Ory remained still.

"He's all yours, Marshal."

Cogan was making his way inside the planation when he heard, "You sent Lezin after me."

Cogan smiled, "Yes. I'm surprised he didn't find you."

"He did. And he won't be coming back." Ory walked with the marshal down the stairs of the plantation as he continued, "But I have no doubt you'll meet again. All three of us maybe."

Ory walked away from the plantation. His hands were chained and so were his ankles, leaving only enough space to walk, as armed men, lead by the marshal, escorted him toward the levee. Toward the river. Its distance from the plantation seemed shorter than ever. The wall grew in front of him. A hard wind blew in his face, rolling over the levee from the river. It seemed that he'd have to face it one last time. As he climbed up the barrier to the top, a tree began to appear. The higher he climbed, the more was revealed. Its branches grew wider, the leaves became thicker, until the tree's trunk came into view. It was a lone cypress with a single bare branch stretching along the canvass of black water behind it. From that branch hung a rope. A noose. The wind was stronger on the river side. White caps were scattered across the river's body. Ory took a few steps down the other side of the levee then collapsed to his knees. He watched the rope swing and the waves crash.

"Just a little more," he whispered. One of the men tried to pick him up, but stopped when Ory said louder, "Just a little more."

The man looked to the marshal, who nodded back to him, and the man left Ory there, giving him some time. Ory let his back fall to the ground. He was losing hope. The image of his sister chained to the river had become more visible. He lay there looking up to the sky. There were no stars. There was no moon. There was no light.

Cogan was back inside the planation, sitting at his desk, waiting for word that it had been done. He pulled out a cigar from a box on his desk. There was a candle lit on the corner of his desk and he leaned in, holding his cigar to it, and after a few puffs, was reclined back in his chair surrounded in smoke. He picked up the deed to all of Ory's land. Being that there was no male left in their family, Cogan enjoyed what he saw coming to him.

His peaceful moment was disturbed by his door slowly opening. It was Bernice and she came steadily in. Cogan rolled his eyes and puffed his cigar, throwing the deed back on the desk. "What now, Bernice?"

"I would like to ask you again. What is to happen to Ory's family?"

"It doesn't concern you."

"Well, maybe it concerns them." Turning to the open door, "You can come in."

From the hall entered Titaunt and Sidonie, huddled close together.

"Maybe you won't mind telling them."

Cogan coughed on his smoke and put his cigar in the tray on his desk. He collected himself and stood. "Ladies. I am truly sorry for your loss."

Neither Titaunt nor Sidonie looked comforted, they were terrified more than anything else. Bernice could not waste time.

"They think you should take all of Ory's land. And I agree."

Cogan's eyes went wide and he shook his head, making sure he heard right. He coughed and said, "Absolutely. I think it might be for the best to have someone like myself to—"

"And you should pay them for it."

Cogan looked to Bernice, smiled, and lowered his head. He laughed for a moment. He picked up his cigar and walked around to the front of his desk. "You know that I don't have to do that. And frankly, it may not be a wise choice, given the family history. I actually have the papers right here." Cogan turned his back to them and placed his cigar down, looking around his desk. "Now, I think we can all agree, legally—"

He heard a click. When he turned around, Bernice was standing right on top of him as she pressed the Colt to his head. Still muddy and ashy, and full of gunpowder.

"I'm sorry, Daddy."

Cogan saw the other Colt in its holster, hanging over a nearby chair. He tried to turn, but the second he did, she pushed the gun harder, digging into his skull.

"Don't think I won't do it. God, I love you, but I'll do it."

Bernice had a wild look in her eyes that even frightened the ladies. It was a look that her father had never seen, and it terrified him.

"I hoped that I could save him. That I could get you to let him go. But I understand it's out of your hands, and it's more than just you that has a hold on him. The river has him now."

Sidonie buried her face in Titaunt's arms as the standoff continued.

"Pay them."

Cogan hesitated, but he eventually moved to the safe behind his desk. He reluctantly opened the door and pulled out a few stacks of bound bills.

"All of it."

"Bernice."

"All of it."

Cogan turned back to the safe and pulled everything out, bills, papers, and all. He hugged them all close to his chest and dumped them on top of his desk.

"You can't give me Ory, so you give me this. They're leaving the River Road. And you will never see them again. And if you don't, if you fail at this, if you go after them, Daddy, I swear to you I will kill myself and you will have done it. It will be as easy as breathing for me and I will do it at the slightest hint."

Cogan didn't like that deal, and though his dark desires continued to grow, he loved his daughter, and would do as she wished.

He said, "Take it and leave."

Titaunt approached the desk, taking slow, small steps, setting her eyes on all the money before her. The stack was high. She thought of Ory. She thought of her sister. Titaunt said in a cracked voice, "This place is what killed him."

Titaunt picked up the deed from across his desk and admired it. She looked down and saw the smoke from the cigar swirling around the desk, and then noticed the candle on the corner. She held the paper to the flame and it caught fire.

Cogan yelled, "What are you doing?"

Bernice looked on. She normally would have had the same reaction, but she had given up thinking she knew what was best for others. Cogan reached to grab the deed out of her hands, but stopped when he heard Bernice. "Cogan."

Her stare held even more power than the gun she held on him. She would do it if she had to. The flames were burning closer to Titaunt's hand as the pale parchment rolled, turning black, but she remained still. She said, "It will never bring them back."

Titaunt held the magnolia necklace that was now back around her neck and threw the burning document on top of the desk and watched the flames roll across the table, consuming the money, and melting the sticks of red wax, creating a bloody pool that crawled into the bills. Titaunt grabbed Sidonie and ran out of the room.

Bernice and her father were all that was left. They stared at each other as the fire between them grew. And when the top of the desk was completely inflamed, she threw the Colt to the ground and never looked into her father's eyes again.

Bernice came out of the plantation, walking down the stairs slowly and stately as men came rushing in after screams of a fire from within. She met Titaunt and Sidonie who sat on the back of a packed wagon, ready to depart for their journey.

"The boat will be waiting where I told you. It leaves tonight, but they're expecting you. It won't take long."

Titaunt thought of the last time that she and Bernice had spoken, and of the words exchanged. She wished she could take some of those back now.

"You should meet us."

Bernice was quick to respond as her mind was on the other side of the levee. "He'll come after me." Bernice handed a letter to Titaunt. "When she's ready, Ory wanted her to know this."

Bernice turned to leave and Sidonie yelled, "What does the letter say?"

Bernice looked down at her eager face. "That your brother loves you. And you should be proud of who you are."

Bernice left them and made her way toward the river. She never looked back to Titaunt, who was now thinking she would have been happy to see her as Ory's wife. They watched her leave and when she could no longer be seen, they started riding down the road.

Sidonie asked, "Where will the boat take us?"

"Home."

Behind them, flames were coming through the windows of the plantation. Sidonie had Ory's watch cradled in her hands. She held her golden gift as the world she knew was burning before her. Her thumb circled along the polished rim of its door, as Ory had done for many years. She pressed the button and looked at her mother's portrait, feeling a growing comfort inside her. Her eyes drifted to the clock, whose hands were still frozen and unmoving. She shook the watch and looked back to its face. Nothing. Her tiny fingers felt a small knob on the side of the watch and began to turn it. When it would turn no more she looked again, watching to see if it would move. Still, nothing. It would seem that Sidonie would have to hold onto it the same way Ory did.

But just before she looked up to the plantation again, she felt a pulse in her hand, and the clock began to click. They rode away, never looking back, out into the darkness, and were never seen again.

Bernice was getting closer to the levee, and as the wall grew in front of her, so did the water in her eyes and the cries in her lungs. She didn't know how much longer she could be strong for them. She came to the levee and stopped, and while she was completely alone, she fell to her knees and cried, letting out a few short screams, then breathed. She knew what was on the other side, only she didn't know if it had happened yet. She wiped her face and got to her feet, took a deep breath and began to walk up the slope. As she approached the top, she, too, saw the tree. With each step she took, more of the tree came into view, gradually exposing its slender trunk. Then that single branch appeared, and then the rope, and she followed it down until the noose appeared. Empty. She had made it to the top and there she saw Ory, still lying on his back. A man came running up the levee to see the planation burning in the distance. The man yelled back to the marshal, "It's on fire. The whole thing is burning."

A few men left, running back toward the plantation. Bernice walked down to Ory. This was easier when she had played it out in her head. She stood in front of him, caught by his green eyes, and wished she hadn't come. It was silent at first, then Ory closed his eyes and asked, "Is she safe?"

"Yes. When the sun rises, they'll be gone."

Ory let out a long exhale and opened his eyes. "Thank you." Ory rolled to his side, pushing himself up with his chained hands and feet. "You should go. If you see this, it'll never leave your mind."

"As if it won't already?"

He looked back to Bernice and he thought again about that life with her, somewhere far from here, living like his father, a man who loved. She watched him as his hand floated toward his side and gently pulled from his pocket the handkerchief she'd given him. He rubbed his fingers across what was once smooth and clean, but now was stained from the grains of red dirt and blood. He had kept it with him, holding it tight through the final days of his journey.

She asked him, "What do you say to someone when you know it's the last time you'll speak to them?"

"You say goodbye."

He put the handkerchief back into his pocket. He would keep it with him still. Ory turned to the river and a golden glow caught his eyes. He stared out at it for a moment, then walked towards the water.

"Where are you going, boy?"

Ory didn't hear the marshal and he continued down to the bank of the river. There was a small dock that stretched far out over the water. Ory stepped onto it and he began to feel the same sensation he did when all those dreams of the long hall came to him, drawing him deep inside the tunnel, pulling him toward the door. Ory walked along the dock until he made it all the way to the end, and all that was before him was black water and golden flames from the plantation reflecting off the top.

Bernice came down and stood at the other end of the dock and yelled, "Wait."

She stood paralyzed, as if she hit an invisible gate at the entrance to the dock. She yelled the first thing that came to her. "We can run."

Even now, a part of Bernice still hoped for her fairytale ending. And a part of her knew it wouldn't happen. Bernice breathed, shut her eyes and laughingly cried. She opened her eyes calmly, her smile aging into a gentle remembrance. Then she spoke firmly. Hopeful. "They're waiting for you. It's all been arranged. She's waiting right now for you to come and take her away from here. She's been waiting all her life for you."

An ease came to Ory's face, then the hall and the door in front of him disappeared. There was only the golden light. And as Ory stared hard out into the distance, the glimmering flames of the planation turned into the roaring fire of the barn, back in the town of the red dirt road. He found himself kneeling again, facing the flames that consumed his friend. A smile grew. As the barn crumbled and collapsed, Ory turned from the flames and into the shadows of the woods around him. He was drawn to a certain darkness, and there he lingered for a moment until he saw him. He saw him there, standing like a lion in the grass, with his wooden weapon in his hand.

Back on the dock he said to the river, "We can't fail each other now. Not after we've come so far."

Ory gently shook his head, looking back up to Will hidden in the woods, a friend ready to give his life. Then with a silent word, Ory said, "Go."

Will disappeared. Free. All that was left was the shadow. The black water of the river. Ory looked down to the chains on his wrists and ankles. Bernice never turned away. She stood firm. Then Ory lifted his head to the river once more.

"Now we're both free, Will."

Ory took one more step and was gone.

THE LAST TO CLIMB

Sometimes he forgot how impossible it was. How much they went through. He remained in the graveyard, the cross at his feet was clean now. He had pulled the weeds from around its base and removed the dirt from its etchings. It read, *Ory L. Fortune*. He was sorry it took him so long. He figured now he would've been long forgotten and that no one would have recognized an old man like him. He knelt down before the cross and placed flowers that he had picked on the grave. He kissed the palm of his hand and pressed it to the earth.

"Goodbye, old friend."

When his hand left the ground he turned his palm up, rubbing the center of it, rubbing the scar from a cut he had given himself many years ago.

Will pressed hard against his cane and brought himself to his feet. As he gave one last look to his friend below, his eyes drew to a cross next to Ory's. The cross had no name. It only read, *I'll look for you on the horizon.* Will's eyes closed and a gentle smile came to him.

He threw his coat over his shoulder, walked out of the graveyard and through the sugar cane, continuing freely down to the River Road. His pace began to slow with each step he took among the tall green stalks. His breath grew short. His body felt heavy. Will looked up and could see the road in the distance. Once he got to it, he stood face to face with the levee. He looked left down one end of the road, seeing it bend and disappear in the distance. He looked right and saw the same. He coughed into his jacket. Will gathered his strength, threw his coat onto the ground, crossed the road, and reached out to climb the levee. He placed both hands on his cane, hooking the ground little by little, pulling himself up the barrier. As he got higher, he could see the top of a tree from the other side. More and more of the tree came into view as he climbed, until he reached the top and saw the lone slender cypress. Tall and bright and full of life.

Will took a few steps down the other side of the levee then sat himself down. His head lowered, unable to look on the river. He was breathing heavy, in short little bursts. A few inhales later, his breath went steady. His heartbeat calmed. Will's head slowly rose, and for the first time in many years, he looked upon the river. A river that was nothing like he remembered. The water was smooth. The sun shone on all its bends and banks, leaving no shadow to be seen. Maybe he had become too romantic in his older days. But still, he opened his eyes and saw a world changed, where some would no longer tolerate the hold the river had on them, pulling back its watery fingers, releasing themselves from its grasp.

The people on the River Road never knew the truth about Ory and Will. No one knew of their innocence, and no one ever knew Ory's father wasn't the killer they thought him to be. Ory would never live there to be thanked for the slaying of the dragon among them. He wouldn't do what they all had hoped, to make the plantation stronger, following the steps of their design. Instead, to them, he would die young, beaten by the River Road, following in the footsteps of his father. He died a murderer and a criminal and that was what they all believed.

In time, their myth would finally fade. Though Will never saw Ory again, he thought he could feel him. Living out lives far from the other, far from the River Road, each still bringing the other hope. He lived content with the fleeting moments of peace that came now and again. Death held Will at one point, but let him go. And he waited a long time before he came again. Then, as Will lay his back on the side of the levee, he felt a storm rage in some dark land far from there. His heart began to beat with its thunder, pounding with each rolling rumble. He felt that Ory had lay there before, feeling that they were somehow reunited again. And as the lightning from that distant storm crashed, Will took his final breath and let out a giant roar that was forever carried along the River Road, and somewhere out in that dark world, the light and the lion were born again.